How long—if ever—had it been since she'd let go?

How hard had it been to keep all this bottled inside? He couldn't imagine. Being one of seven, he was never at a loss for a confidant.

However, he wasn't stubborn J. J. Barnes who thought anything less than absolute competence was a sign of weakness. It was probably killing her to be held and comforted, but he didn't care. She needed it.

It was some time before she began to pull out of his embrace. Reluctantly he let her go.

"Better?"

She smiled weakly. "Not really. No."

"I can hold you some more."

Her smile broadened. "Using you as a crutch is a great way to solve my problems."

"I'm really sorry about—"

"Don't apologize. The Visnopovs can't hurt me anymore. I've got you for protection, so what could possibly happen?"

Dear Reader,

Happy holidays! Or as I like to think of it—the busiest time of the year! So, thanks for taking time out of your hectic schedule to read *Charmed and Dangerous*.

This book was a challenge, and not for the reasons you might think. In the middle of telling Cody and J.J.'s story, Mother Nature played a very cruel trick on me—twice! Hurricanes Frances and Jeanne came to visit. I must share my incredible respect and gratitude to all the volunteers, friends, agencies and neighbors who pulled together to help us put our lives back together.

U.S. Marshal Cody Landry has met his match in this book and J. J. Barnes wastes little time making sure he understands that. She's not his average protectee and he isn't quite sure how to deal with the situation— or with her. Fundamentally, this is a story about trust. Avoiding it, sharing it, losing it and finding your way back to it again. It helps that Cody is a Landry. The strong Landry family bonds are always impressive to the women drawn into this world. But they can also be daunting. Especially at this point in the series— with five of the brothers now married, J.J. needs a score card to remember who is who.

We're at the home stretch now. *Charmed and Dangerous* brings you a step closer to discovering the Landry secret. I hope you enjoy the book! Please feel free to contact me at www.KelseyRoberts.net or through Harlequin at www.eHarlequin.com, or the old-fashioned way, c/o Harlequin Books, 233 Broadway, 10th Floor, New York, New York, 10279.

All the best!

Kelsey Roberts

KELSEY ROBERTS

CHARMED AND DANGEROUS

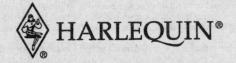

HARLEQUIN®

TORONTO • NEW YORK • LONDON
AMSTERDAM • PARIS • SYDNEY • HAMBURG
STOCKHOLM • ATHENS • TOKYO • MILAN • MADRID
PRAGUE • WARSAW • BUDAPEST • AUCKLAND

For the wonderful girls in my life—my beautiful Katie Scarlett, adorable Paige Elizabeth and growing-up-too-fast Blysse Lara! You fill the future with the promise of loves to come.

ACKNOWLEDGMENT

This book would not have been possible without Marshal Mike! Thanks so much for sharing your time and expertise with me and I really appreciate you letting my mother meet her first felon.

ISBN 0-373-22886-4

CHARMED AND DANGEROUS

Copyright © 2005 by Rhonda Harding Pollero

This edition published by arrangement with Harlequin Books S.A.

® and TM are trademarks of the publisher. Trademarks indicated with ® are registered in the United States Patent and Trademark Office, the Canadian Trade Marks Office and in other countries.

www.eHarlequin.com

Printed in U.S.A.

ABOUT THE AUTHOR

Kelsey Roberts has penned more than twenty novels, won numerous awards and nominations, and landed on bestseller lists, including *USA TODAY* and the Ingrams Top 50 List. She has been featured in the *New York Times* and the *Washington Post,* and makes frequent appearances on both radio and television. She is considered an expert in why women read and write crime fiction, as well as an excellent authority on plotting and structuring the novel.

She resides in south Florida with her family.

Books by Kelsey Roberts

HARLEQUIN INTRIGUE

*The Rose Tattoo
†The Landry Brothers

CAST OF CHARACTERS

Cody Landry—This former Montana state policeman has been desperately trying to find his missing parents, but now his mission is to keep the lovely J. J. Barnes safe…any way he can.

J. J. Barnes—She's had quite a history with Cody and wouldn't turn to him if she had any choice. But with the Russian mob gunning for her, she must take the protection Cody offers.

Martin Newell—What is this U.S. Marshal hiding? And will it cost J. J. her life?

Lara Selznick—This female U.S. Marshal has a lot to prove. What lengths will that need drive her to?

Alex Moslonovis—A mob witness with a giant target painted on his head.

Goran Visnopov—This Russian mob boss wants J. J. dead. And he always gets what he wants.

Chapter One

"I don't need a baby-sitter, due respect, sir. I am fully capable of taking care of myself." J.J. Barnes was not happy, and she made sure her narrowed glare made that point. The barely healed scar on her right side itched and pulled. Maybe tomorrow she could compartmentalize and put the incident behind her once and for all.

Calmly seated behind his desk, FBI Associate Director Terrance "Red" Andrews didn't seem impressed by her rhetoric. In fact, his white brows arched cautioningly in response to her tone.

J.J. immediately adjusted her attitude. Outwardly, at least. Inside, her stomach churned as waves of queasiness rocked through her. She covered by leaning forward to grip the back of the burgundy leather chair as if to argue the point.

"You've been reinstated to full duty, Agent Barnes. But that doesn't solve the immediate problem." He peered up at her over the rims of his half-glasses, his blue eyes stern and unyielding. "I would assume that after the Visnopov debacle, you'd be more...circumspect."

"I am, sir," she assured him. "Two weeks in the

hospital and a month recuperating at home gave me plenty of time to analyze my actions. I realize now that I should have arranged for backup prior to the meeting."

"It wasn't a *meeting,* Agent Barnes. It was a beating. The government has invested a great deal of time and money in this investigation. We'd like you to stay alive until the U.S. Attorney gets in front of a grand jury. Understood?"

"Yes, sir."

Andrews shuffled papers around on his cluttered desk until he found a thin folder and held it out for her. "You *will* accept a protective detail."

"But, sir—"

He lifted a finger, silencing her immediately. He smiled, his expression somewhere between grudging respect and utter exasperation. "Sit, Barnes."

She readily followed the order. She was still sore from the surgery. She didn't know much about having a spleen removed, but she guessed the fatigue that just refused to go away no matter how many hours she slept was a side effect. J.J. prided herself on her fitness. She was the reigning female record holder on the obstacle course and now she was having trouble making it through the day without a nap.

She took the folder, but she didn't open it immediately. It was accepted practice to wait for a superior's go-ahead before diving into anything. If she'd followed that procedure, maybe Visnopov's goons wouldn't have—

"I know you, Barnes," he said, raking his stubby fingers through his thick shock of white hair. "I knew you'd balk at the idea of protection, so I came up with an incentive for you."

Her mood brightened slightly. "Sir?"

Nodding, he pointed at the folder. "We've lost three critical Visnopov witnesses so far," he began as she perused color photos of the victims. "You were almost the fourth."

J.J. wasn't sure how to react. She could have argued that the three witnesses killed thus far weren't her fault. Her cover was blown the minute the first member of Visnopov's crew was arrested. It would have been nice if the U.S. Attorney coordinated the arrest with the bureau. Given her a heads-up. But arguing—in Andrews's eyes—conveyed a complete lack of personal responsibility and she wasn't about to give him any more reasons to question her abilities.

"The Visnopovs are going to come after you again."

A frisson of dread slid down her spine. She straightened her back and kept her gaze steady with effort. "I assumed as much."

"The Marshal's Service will handle the particulars."

A groan escaped her lips before she could prevent it. J.J. hoped Andrews hadn't noticed it as she flipped to the next photo, her interest instantly piqued. This wasn't a picture of a criminal or a victim. This was an official head shot of a U.S. marshal. Turning to the back of the photograph, she read the particulars. Denise Howard, fifty-one, twenty-five years with the Service. "She's my protective detail?"

"Not exactly," Andrews said as she continued to examine the file.

Martin Newell, forty-nine. Lara Selznick, twenty-six, who looked more like a college coed than a federal agent. The last picture made J.J.'s heart skip. He was as handsome as she remembered. "But…" She glanced up at Andrews and said, "I don't follow, sir. These people are—"

"Suspects in the murder of Alex Maslonovic," Andrews explained. "We have every reason to believe that someone inside the U.S. marshal's office is a mole. Your assignment is to find out which one of them is responsible."

"I'M SUPPOSED TO TRY to get her killed, too?" Cody Landry didn't bother to mask his sarcasm. Partly because he'd known the field director long enough to speak freely and partly because he was really, seriously pissed.

He stared across the table, meeting the other man's calm, even expression. As always, George Avery was immune to Cody's temper. "Nobody's supposed to *get* killed. Besides, it isn't like she's a civilian," George pointed out. "She's a highly trained federal agent."

Cody knew all about J.J. Barnes. She was one of those women who sometimes crossed the line between being assertive and being a bitch. They'd been at Quantico together for a three-month course, and J.J. had done everything in her power to prove she was equal, or better, than any man there. He felt a smile twitch his lips. The only problem was that no one—male or female— could ever mistake J.J. for anything other than a woman. She had a sensuality that couldn't be hidden by any amount of attitude. In a word, she was hot, and she'd shot him down at every turn.

"She's very…competent," Cody allowed.

His cautious tone elicited a smirk from George. "I've seen her file. She's gorgeous."

"If you like 'em tall, blond and leggy."

George laughed aloud. "As I recall, you do."

Cody sighed before taking a pull from his bottle of beer. *Why did it have to be her?* "You do remember I'm scheduled for a thirty-day leave, right?"

George nodded. "I was hoping you'd postpone. This is important, Cody. The A.G. told the FBI. Then someone in the FBI blew her cover and nearly got her killed. This ruse is the only way the feebs think they can flush out the leak."

"Since when is it our responsibility to clean *their* house?"

"Since blowing her cover cost us three protectees. Like it or not—and I don't—we're in this together and dangling J.J. Barnes out on a limb is our best chance at finding the leak and making sure the rest of the witnesses live long enough to testify against Visnopov and his crew."

J.J.'s face loomed in Cody's mind's eye. "She's very smart, George. I'm guessing it will take her about a minute to figure out that she's being used."

"Her boss says different," George insisted. "He concocted some story about her investigating *us.*"

"I'm not your guy for this," Cody argued, finishing his beer as he started to rise. "I'm going home. I've got four nieces and nephews I haven't met yet and another brother is getting married. I'm not missing another family event."

"We can work around that," George insisted. "You can take J.J. and the team with you."

Cody froze. "You want me to take a woman with a target painted on her forehead around my family? I'll pass, thanks."

George stood so quickly that his chair tilted backward before crashing against the bar's scuffed wooden floor. Reaching into the breast pocket of his jacket, he produced a rumpled sheet of paper. "I've arranged for a safe house outside of Jasper. It's perfect, Cody. You can kill two birds with one stone."

Cody rolled his eyes at the inappropriate choice of words. "I'm taking my time off, George." He slapped a couple of bills on the table. "I've earned it, requisitioned it, filled out all the forms in triplicate and, by God, I'm taking it." He gave his boss and friend a pointed look and said flatly, *"Alone,"* before he turned and headed for the door.

He knew Avery would follow him even without a backward glance. Grabbing his jacket from its hook, he shoved open the wooden front door and allowed the crisp November air to hit his face. His SUV was parked beneath the lone flickering street lamp near the back of the parking lot.

He listened to the chorus of city sounds coming across the Potomac. The buzz of traffic and shrill horns emanating from an unending ribbon of headlights only solidified his determination. He needed out of D.C. for a while. Needed to see the stars and hear the quiet waiting for him in Montana. He was a fish out of water in the east. No, not just the east—in a city, surrounded by throngs of people and...*things*. It seemed as if every square inch of land was occupied in some fashion. Even vacant lots were fenced, and the fences used as bulletin boards. The air smelled of exhaust and the briny polluted river that edged the nation's capitol.

Yanking open his car, Cody instantly spied the envelope on the driver's seat. He knew what it was.

George arrived a few seconds later, huffing out labored breaths that condensed into temporary clouds. "Your flight leaves in the morning. She'll be waiting for you in Helena along with your team."

On principle, Cody refused to open the envelope. "I said no, George. Doesn't that matter?"

"Not so much," he replied, placing a hand on Cody's shoulder and giving a squeeze. "You can either have a working vacation or no vacation at all."

Annoyed, Cody tossed the envelope onto the passenger's seat. "Thanks, that's kind of like asking me to pick my favorite Menendez brother."

George's hand lingered, then fell away as Cody locked his gaze on him. At least his boss tried to look apologetic.

"I know this is a tough break, Cody. But it's necessary. The Visnopov case is a top priority."

"I get that," Cody snapped, also knowing full well that his sense of duty was about to rear its ugly head.

"Drugs, money laundering, prostitution, guns, numbers, extortion—they're a one-stop shopping crime empire," George continued. "We need all the remaining witnesses alive if the U.S. Attorney has a hope of getting convictions. That includes J.J. Barnes. She gathered a lot of information during her two years undercover and they know it, thanks to the leak. They need her dead and they've got inside help."

Shrugging away from George, Cody slipped inside the car. "I should quit, George."

"But you won't."

"But I should. I *definitely* should."

J.J. WAS HAVING a bad day. No, make that a horrible day. And a long one. She'd spent two hours in a small, private room at the airport in New York under the watchful eye of U.S. Marshal Denise Howard. The marshal wasn't exactly an interesting traveling companion. In fact, the woman was aloof, almost to the point of rudeness. During the required preflight waiting period in New York, the leg from New York to Chicago, the two-hour layover in Chicago and now, fifty-seven minutes into the flight to Helena, Denise had been practically mute.

J.J. was far from thrilled with this assignment, but she had a job to do. One that would be much easier if Denise had a few social skills.

Shifting in the confining seat, J.J. angled to study the woman. She looked like a marshal, thanks to a drab navy pantsuit and simple white blouse. There were deep concentration lines at the corners of her brown eyes, traces of coral lipstick on her mouth, and a swipe of some peachy shadow on her lids—barely enough to qualify as makeup. She smelled of soap and peppermint and, most of the time, her attention was fixed on the financial page displayed on the laptop she'd set up on the tray table.

"How's the Dow?" J.J. asked. She didn't really care; she was just desperate for conversation to cut the boredom.

"Weak," Denise answered without looking up.

Matching your interpersonal skills. "I need to use the ladies' room."

Her comment earned her an annoyed glance from Denise. "We'll be landing soon."

"Not soon enough," J.J. insisted.

Denise huffed as she closed the laptop, stowed it in her briefcase and eventually slipped out of the seat. A fairly easy task for Denise, who couldn't have been more than five-four. J.J. was a good five to six inches taller and still stiff and sore from her surgery. Navigating the narrow space between the seats was nothing short of an athletic achievement.

Like the two earlier times, Denise followed her up the aisle and watched diligently as J.J. closed the door and slid the latch. The strong smell of cherry odorizer didn't exactly make her queasy stomach happy. A minute later, as she washed her hands, she felt the plane begin to descend at the same time the Return to Seat light began to flash.

Denise began to rap on the door. Apparently the woman was as patient as she was friendly. "Be right there!" J.J. called.

She checked her reflection, combing through her hair with her fingers, then reached down to check the phone and weapon holstered in identical ankle straps tucked into her socks and hidden by the legs of her slacks. Traveling with a U.S. marshal had allowed her to by-pass the security measures that would easily have detected the gun. Her status as an FBI agent had allowed her to wave off Denise's attempt to pat her down.

"I wouldn't have made that mistake," she muttered.

"How much longer did you say this would take?" Denise called from the other side of the door.

J.J. unlatched the door, emerging to find Denise and a flight attendant giving her dirty looks. She quickly moved through the one-quarter filled plane and found her small seat. Again, she twisted and sidestepped her way back into position before sitting and fastening her lap belt. "It would have been nice to fly first-class," she commented when her knees hit the seatback in front of her.

"Budget cuts," Denise remarked. "We'll wait until all the passengers deplane, then proceed to—"

"I know the drill," J.J. interrupted.

"The DIC will be waiting at…"

J.J. found it perversely funny that the acronym for Deputy-Marshal-In-Charge so closely matched her opinion of Cody Landry. Of course, the word she was thinking had an extra letter and wasn't something she'd say aloud, but the mere thought made her smile. Probably for the last time. She was dreading the notion of seeing him again.

Thirty minutes later, she realized why.

THE MAN SWAGGERED! Aside from John Wayne—who was paid to swagger—what kind of man swaggered?

Cody Landry. Tall, dark, handsome Cody Landry.

She hated that her heart tensed at the first sight of him. Intellectually she knew it was nothing more than a chemical reaction, coded into her DNA. He was a gorgeous guy, so it made perfect sense that her body would react to him. But that didn't mean she had to like it.

Or the brilliant smile he flashed. Or his eyes that were the color of chocolate. Or the lock of thick, jet-black hair that had fallen across his deeply tanned forehead, making her positively itch to reach out and tuck it back into place.

This is not starting out well, she thought as she extended her hand and willed herself not to moan when his fingers closed over hers.

"Agent Barnes, we meet again."

J.J. frowned. "We've met befo…" She allowed the question to trail off, paused three beats, then feigned an oh yeah, now I remember moment. "Right. Quantico a few years ago for that document course, if I'm remembering correctly."

His smile slipped fractionally and he released her hand. "It was a twelve-week course on surveillance technology, actually." Another woman and man appeared as if on cue. "This is Deputy Marshal Martin Newell and—" he paused while J.J. shook the man's hand "—Deputy Marshal Lara Selznick."

Cody was trying to get a read on J.J. And not succeeding all that well. It seemed that all his mind wanted to process was the fact that she was even more stunning than he remembered. Her blond hair was longer and looked as if she'd recently run her fingers through it. Because of her height, he could look almost directly into her eyes. Her incredible eyes. They weren't blue or green, but a blend of the two colors that didn't seem possible in nature.

His cool professionalism nearly slipped when he noticed the faint remnants of a bruise on her right cheek. As far as he could see, it was the only visible reminder of the beating she'd taken at the hands of Visnopov's goons.

"We'll be exiting at air cargo," he explained, pointing the way. It took everything in him not to put his hand at the small of her back to guide her as he would have any other woman. Any other woman who wasn't a) a feeb, b) a total tight ass, and c) ruining his first vacation —and homecoming—in six years.

And d) she hadn't even *remembered* him, he thought as he walked beside her. Well, hell. This was going to be really special.

Not.

Per their training, the deputies surrounded her as they moved through the public area of the terminal. "Our location is approximately—"

"May I stop at the rest room?"

Ignoring Denise's groan of displeasure, Cody nodded and steered everyone toward the detour. Lara and Denise entered the rest room with J.J., leaving Cody and Martin to guard the lone entrance.

"She's a looker."

"She's an assignment," Cody reminded Martin. "And believe me, beneath that pretty exterior is a very unpleasant person."

Martin shrugged. "Seems nice enough."

"Just wait. Agent Barnes has issues."

"With looks like that, she could have scurvy and I wouldn't care."

Cody glanced in Martin's direction. "Aren't you married, old friend?"

"I'm only lusting in my mind, Cody. That's not prohibited in the marriage vows."

"Should I call your wife and ask her?"

Martin shook his head. "Let's keep it between us men for now. No need upsetting my woman."

Of course J.J. chose that moment to emerge from the rest room. She immediately tossed both men a scathing look.

"Don't get yourself in a knot," he warned J.J. as they continued toward their destination. "We were just making small talk."

"About the ownership of women?" she replied with an angry dose of sarcasm. "That's illegal, Deputy Marshal Landry. You should have read that somewhere by this point in your career."

"Call me Cody," he replied easily, determined not to bait her further. "Martin was referring to his wife."

"In a demeaning and archaic fashion."

Cody blew out a breath. "I think that's an issue you should take up with him." He quickened the pace toward the black SUV he'd parked twenty long yards ahead.

"You're the…DIC. Isn't it part of your job as team leader to keep sexist references out of the workplace? Under all federal and EEOC guidelines regarding inappropriate content it's your responsibility—"

"Give it a rest, J.J."

"I'm only pointing out that what may seem like an innocent comment between men often is a highly offensive—"

He cut her off by raising one hand and opening the back door of the vehicle with the other. "No one was trying to be offensive to anyone."

"Intent isn't the point," she argued, apparently refusing to get into the car until she'd made her point. Again. "Technically speaking, I could make a formal complaint. You could be investigated, possibly punished in some way."

Cody rolled his eyes. "Technically speaking, J.J., I'm already feeling punished. Now get in the damn car."

Chapter Two

The bathroom was clean.

But just to be absolutely certain, J.J. checked again. She had to be quick. She had to be thorough. She had to be sure. This assignment was too critical to chance being overheard. For the second time she felt along the underside of the sink, then the tub, then any place else she could think where a camera or listening device might be hidden.

Bug free.

Using running water as cover, she silently closed the toilet lid, sat down and pulled the cell phone provided by her boss from its hiding place in her sock. She began crafting her text message.

Arrived. Carver Hunting Lodge. Two-point-seven miles ESE Jasper. Advise re: status background checks. Barnes out.

Satisfied, she hit the envelope icon on the keypad and sent the message to Red, the preprogrammed recipient. A few seconds later, the phone began to vibrate against her palm.

Her boss must have been waiting for her communication. The small screen flashed twice, then revealed his response.

Background checks in progress. Initial assessment?

J.J. rolled her eyes. Did he think she had all the time in the world? Typing on a cell phone was neither fast nor easy.

Nothing obvious. Barnes out.

Exchange over, she put the phone back in her sock. It immediately began to vibrate against her calf. J.J. rolled her eyes again.

This time the message read:

You can bring Landry into the loop if need be.

NO NEED,

She replied furiously and in capitals, the universally understood way of shouting in text form.

Landry can NOT be trusted. Barnes OUT.

She had just flipped the phone closed when Lara began pounding on the door.

"Are you okay, J.J.?"

"Fine!" she called, "be right out!" After stuffing the phone back into place, she yanked down the hem of her pant leg and moved to the vanity. "Ugh," she groaned, then rubbed her cheeks, hoping to offset her pallor. No such luck. Even splashing water on her face didn't do the trick.

"LOOK WHAT THE COLD blew in."

Cody found himself drawn into the back-slapping embrace of his youngest brother, Shane. The Landrys were an affectionate family, courtesy of their mother's loving example. Just thinking about her made Cody's chest tighten.

She'd been gone—missing—for more than a decade. It made him nuts. The not knowing. The scenarios he played in his mind. Not understanding how his mother could just decide—out of the blue—to run off and never look back. Mostly he just missed her. Especially her counsel. Pricilla Landry had always managed to impart quiet wisdom to her sons. In that respect, she was nothing like their father. Caleb was a loud, wildly fun man. Strict to be sure, and a great dad. But he'd chosen to leave with his wife. Overnight, the Landrys had gone from a large, happy *family* to seven young men left to fend for themselves.

Holding Shane at arm's length, Cody smiled at his sibling. Though Shane would never say, Cody was convinced the evaporation of their family had affected his little brother the most. He was the baby—in more ways than chronology. He was the spoiled one. At least by their mother.

Shane shrugged and halfheartedly punched Cody in the arm. "It is so good to have you back. Especially since we're the last two."

"The last two what?" Cody asked, as he walked

through the foyer toward the kitchen, loving the familiar scents of the family home. Even though the pie he smelled hadn't been baked by his mother, it still poignantly reminded him of coming home after school to the tantalizing fragrances of hot apple and cinnamon. His heart pinched.

"Independent men," Shane answered, following on his heels. "This place is all about women and wedding stuff and babies and—"

"Stop whining," Taylor Reese huffed before slipping the delicious-smelling apple pie from the oven and offering Cody a warm smile. "Welcome home, Cody. You have perfect timing. I made this especially for you."

"I thought it was for all of us," Shane grumbled, grabbing a chair, turning it backward and then falling into the seat to glare at his housekeeper.

The same seat, Cody noted, that his brother had occupied for more than thirty years. Even when Shane had been off *finding* himself, his chair stood empty. Waiting for him. As they all had.

Taylor, clad in jeans and a very attractive snug red shirt, parked her hands on her hips and offered the youngest Landry brother a withering glare. "This isn't a democracy. You whine, you don't get dessert."

"It's a dictatorship," Shane retorted, sounding very much like a six-foot-four-inch child. "I'm your employer, you can't deny me food."

Taylor dismissed the order with a sarcastic little grunt and a tilt of her head. Several strands of dark blond hair fell loose from her ponytail as her gaze bore into Shane.

Cody's interest was piqued. He sensed tension...the kind that connected a man and a woman valiantly battling any sort of connection.

Smiling to himself, he took his seat and wondered how long his baby brother had been hot for the fetching young housekeeper.

"Sam is my employer. *You* are a pain in my...toe." Taylor went to the fridge and grabbed two bottles of beer. She handed Cody one, then practically threw the other at Shane. "I'm sorry, Cody, I'd love to stay and chat, but I've got a final exam next week, so I've got to study." She managed to wipe down the countertop and finish loading the dishwasher as she spoke.

"The pie needs to cool for about a half hour." She opened a cabinet and took out a plate, then folded a paper towel as a napkin and laid it and a fork on the table beside the pie. "Help yourself. There's homemade vanilla ice cream in the freezer." Then, after her tornado of activity, the tiny woman disappeared from the room..

Cody smiled as they watched her exit. "Is she always so frenetic?" he asked as soon as he heard Taylor's footfalls fade.

Not smiling, Shane nodded, taking a long pull on his beer. "And irritating. And mouthy. And pushy. And—"

"Nice body, though," Cody remarked on a sigh.

"Killer body," Shane agreed readily. "She'd be a dream woman if you could find a way to glue her mouth closed."

Cody chuckled. "Wouldn't you be bored with a woman who didn't speak her mind?"

"I used to think so," Shane admitted, leaning his

chair forward on two legs as he traced the beer label with his thumbnail. "Living with Taylor has made me think I might prefer someone mute."

Letting out a slow whistle, Cody realized his brother was only making the comment as a defensive posture. Thanks to his handy wireless PDA and regular e-mails from brother Seth's wife Savannah, he knew all about the Shane-is-in-love-with-Taylor-and-won't-admit-it-to-himself situation.

"She seems nice," Cody commented, pretty much just to bait Shane. That was part and parcel of being a Landry brother. Shane was the perpetual target. Most of the time deservedly so.

"So did Roy's white tiger and look where that got him."

Cody grinned. The man protested too much. This situation could provide some excellent entertainment while he was here. Reaching for his beer, he noticed the large bruise on his brother's forearm. Poor bastard bruised at the drop of a hat. "What've you been doing?"

Shane glanced down at the purple mark and shrugged. "I bought a new horse. He's not exactly taking an instant liking to me."

"Maybe if you sent flowers or—" Cody had to duck to avoid the spoon Shane launched in his direction. It clattered on the floor and the two of them shared almost boyish grins before everything on and around the table became a projectile. Whoever said you could never go home again wasn't a Landry.

Ten minutes later, Sam entered the kitchen, looked around and shook his head. "What are you guys? Six?"

Sam Landry was holding his sleeping son in his arms. Not an easy task since the boy was almost seven and, from the looks of him, a decent-size kid.

Sam's wife, Callie, simply nodded from the doorway, her arms full with baby Sheldon, a diaper bag and her purse. In a loud whisper, she called, "Welcome home. I've got to put these guys to bed."

"Need help?" Cody asked.

"We've got it down to a science," Sam said easily. "Give me a minute and one of you grab me a beer."

Neither of them did. Something Sam pointed out with greatly exaggerated disgust upon his return. "You guys are useless."

Sam, ever the responsible one, got his beer out of the fridge as well as two more bottles that he placed in the center of the scarred table that had been in the kitchen since the ranch house was built by their grandfather. He raised his bottle in a toast. "To the return of one Landry and the creation of others."

"Again?" Shane asked.

Sam practically puffed out his chest. "I am a virile, manly man compelled to bring forth the fruit of my loins."

"You probably had to get her drunk," Cody teased, tapping bottles with his brother.

"In fact, I am so virile," Sam continued, his eyes filled with unbridled joy, "that my wife carries not one but two of my issues."

"Married to you, I'd say your wife has more than just two issues," Shane joked.

Sam slapped the side of the youngest Landry's head.

"We just met with the builder and asked him to add bed-rooms to the house. So, I'm sorry we weren't here to greet you when you got in."

Cody patted Sam's back. "I'm happy for you. For all of you," he said, meaning it. "Wow, four kids. You're going to be busy."

"It's a good busy," Sam said on a contented breath. "Kevin and Sheldon are great little guys. We're really excited to have more."

"Remember that thought when it's time for work and you've gotten three minutes of sleep," Shane offered. "You're pretty snotty when you don't get enough sleep."

"I'll give you that," Sam said with a single nod of his head. "So what's your excuse, Shane? You've been grumpy for weeks now."

"No sex?" Cody suggested, directing his comment to Sam.

The corners of Sam's mouth quirked into a smile. "Probably. He hasn't had a date in forever. It's the po-nytail. What woman wants a guy with a ponytail?"

"Lots of women," Shane protested.

As always, it amazed Cody how easily his little brother took the bait. "Those would be the same 'lots of women' you *aren't* dating?"

"And your social schedule is full?" Shane tossed back. "The last woman I remember hearing about was some empty-headed receptionist who stalked you when you dumped her. And that was more than a year ago."

Cody cringed at the memory of Mallory. A definite lapse in judgment. At first glance, she'd seemed like an ideal woman for him—outgoing, sweet, very feminine and nurturing. Then, when he didn't propose on the sixth date, she'd thrown an I-want-to-be-married-before-I'm-thirty psychotic fit. After their resulting breakup, she called more than a determined telemarketer and kept turning up at his office, his home, even his gym. He'd been an hour away from getting a restraining order when Mallory turned her attentions onto her next potential husband.

"First of all, I don't tell you about every woman I date. Second of all, I've been busy," Cody said, hearing how very lame that sounded aloud. "Unlike you, I haven't been celibate, so my attitude doesn't need adjusting."

"That's just because the odds were in your favor in D.C.," Shane argued. "The pool of available women is larger in D.C., statistically speaking, so you were bound to find at least one willing person in such a large population base."

"I think he's got you on that one," Sam commented, stifling a yawn.

Cody knew he was supposed to keep up his end of the taunt, but his brain suddenly changed focus without warning to J.J.

"Hello?" Sam called.

It was only then that Cody realized his older brother was standing and about to leave. "Sorry," Cody muttered.

"Are you sure you can't bunk here for the night?" Sam asked. "Callie wants to catch up with you, but she's too tired tonight."

"I'll be in and out," Cody promised. "A working vacation was the best I could swing, unfortunately. Can I use the office computer real quick?"

"Of course," Sam said, obviously annoyed that Cody would ask. "Don't forget about the mandatory dinner tomorrow night. You'll like Molly."

"Almost as much as you'll like seeing Chandler all nuts about her," Shane interjected. "He's completely in love and still trying to convince her that he wasn't the one who shot her."

Cody smiled with a mixture of relief and amusement, remembering the way Molly's ordeal had ended with a blazing shoot-out in the desert. Thankfully only the bad guy had been killed. But in the process, Molly had been grazed by a bullet. And from all accounts, she teasingly continued to hold Chandler responsible for her injury even though no one knew for sure whose bullet struck Molly.

"You can bring a date," Shane mocked.

Like his own private slide show, images of J.J. Barnes flashed again in Cody's mind. He could see her tall, athletic body, and the pretty features she tried so hard to downplay.

"I might at that," he told Shane as he got up from the table. "I've got some work to do," he said absently. "Catch you later."

Why was J.J. so determined not to allow a drop of femininity to slip out? Cody wondered as he left the kitchen. In his experience, being attractive was an asset—probably an unfair generalization, but pretty true nonetheless. And J.J. was a step above pretty. She had those aqua eyes that made his stomach tingle just thinking about them. And her full lips almost begged to be explored. It wasn't fair. No woman who worked so hard to play androgynous should be given that many natural gifts.

He speculated what J.J. would think of his family home, and his brothers. Odd. He'd never brought a woman here. Not that J.J. would be a *date* or anything…

He scrutinized the house as he headed toward Sam's office. A lot had changed in the years he'd been gone. Now the hallways were littered with toys and the walls were adorned with the crayon art of the gaggle of nieces and nephews born in the past few years.

But just as much remained the same. Like the smell of the office. He stepped inside and it was like stepping back in time. He still got a little chill when he entered the dark, richly paneled room. This had been his father's office. Where punishments—great and small—were portioned out. Now, though, thanks either to Taylor or Callie, there were some homey touches. Like the afghan draped over the worn leather chair facing the stone fireplace. And the rug had been replaced—the new one more girlie than the simple rust-and-black thing he'd spilled yellow poster paint on in the third grade.

The changes would probably make his old man crazy. Caleb was a no frills kind of man. So it was probably good that he'd had only sons. Cody couldn't imagine his father raising a daughter. He'd have turned her into…into…J.J. Barnes.

Dammit! Why did the woman keep crawling into his head? he wondered as he fell into the high-backed leather chair behind the desk. It squeaked in protest under his weight and he noted that one of the brass wheels was sticking. He rifled through the desk drawers, found some WD-40 and took care of the chair as the computer booted.

Reaching into his pocket, he retrieved his PDA and a small cable, connected it to the machine, then typed codes to get to the secure server. This was a lot easier and a lot faster than relying on the phone lines back at the safe house.

Where J.J. Barnes was probably taking a bath. Naked.

"As opposed to taking one fully dressed?" he grumbled. But chastising himself didn't prevent his brain from wandering while he waited for his messages to upload to his handheld.

At least he was gentleman enough to make it a bubble bath. Which, in some perversion of gallantry, seemed somehow more sexy than an image of her completely nude. Long, shapely legs peeking out from the water, head tilted back, eyes closed, candles everywhere. He could almost smell scented bath crystals and candle wax as his mind insisted on taunting him. With her head resting against the rim of the tub, blond hair haphazardly pinned up, save for a few wayward strands, he could just imagine the temptation of her neck, how it would feel to run his mouth from the tip of her earlobe all the way down to the outline of her collarbone. He imagined her skin would be soft, warm and—

The computer beeped and flashed Terminated.

Shaking his head, he tried to dispel the fantasies from

his mind. The assignment would be hard enough without lusting after the woman he was meant to protect.

J.J. HAD BATHED and changed into sweats, then joined the others in the main part of the rustic four-bedroom cabin. Lara and Denise were sharing one bedroom while Martin, Cody and J.J. all got singles. Worked for her. This assignment was hard enough without being stuck with a roommate.

Unless the roomy was Cody.

Back up! she yelled at that little voice in her head. To distract herself, she went to the refrigerator and took her time surveying the sparse contents. It was safer than the possibility of one of her jailers reading her thoughts.

They weren't thoughts so much as porn. The short film playing in her mind's eye featured Cody Landry, stripped to the waist, approaching her bed. The image wasn't pure fantasy. She'd seen him in just such a way during their time at Quantico. Only then, she'd been hiding behind a tree trunk, gawking at him like some pathetic coed.

They'd been running the obstacle course at the same time, only he finished first. When she found him at the water station, he'd stripped off his T-shirt and was holding a hose above his head, water cascading down his impressive shoulders.

She'd stopped abruptly, eyes fixed on the sculpted muscles of his broad tanned chest. A thick V of dark hair served as a directional arrow toward his waistband.

Sunlight had glistened off his damp skin as he tossed the hose aside and used his shirt to towel off his face, then his arms, and finally his perfectly chiseled stomach and abdomen.

J.J.'s mouth had gone desert-dry and her heart rate quickened in response to seeing him. Something that had never, *ever* happened to her in all her thirty-two years. Not before or since.

The knowledge inspired irritation, something she took out on the helpless refrigerator, slamming the door so hard she heard bottles clanging inside.

"I need ginger ale," she announced to the group.

"We'll pick some up tomorrow," Martin offered.

J.J. shook her head. "I want some now."

Denise shot her a "spoiled bitch" look while Lara pulled her shoes on. "I'll run to the store. I need some exercise anyway."

"Me, too," J.J. stated, taking two steps toward her room.

"No way," Martin said firmly. "It's dark outside."

J.J. rolled her eyes. "Dark?" she repeated. "What am I, seven?"

Martin's normally placid face morphed into a scowl. "You're a protectee, Barnes. That means no late-night runs. You, either, Selznick. At least not alone."

"Denise?" Lara asked.

The other woman shook her head.

"Martin?"

"Not for two miles in this cold."

Lara offered J.J. an apologetic glance, then returned her attention to the maps she'd been studying. "We can go when Cody comes back."

"When *exactly* is he expected?" J.J. demanded. The only reply was a collective shrug. "Surely he has a cell phone," she suggested. "Call him and ask him to stop for ginger ale on the way back."

"No can do," Martin replied, grabbing the remote control for the small color television and flipping to some sports talk show. "Cody is taking some personal time and he doesn't like to be disturbed for trivial things."

What *kind* of personal time? J.J. wondered, annoyed by his absence. Here she was, *dying* of thirst and needing a ginger ale, and he was off somewhere quite possibly having a quickie.

She pulled herself up short. Where had the real J.J. Barnes gone? Why did *she* care who Cody Landry slept with? It was absolutely none of her business. None. She'd only complicate her job having fantasies about a man she was supposed to be watching for a whole other reason.

Knowing that it would look odd if she thumped her head against the wall, J.J. gave herself a mental thump instead. *Focus on the job.*

Glancing up to find that she hadn't moved, Martin muttered, "I'll go out with Lara as soon as he comes back."

Nice of him to tear himself away from the fascinating commentary about ice hockey blaring from the set.

Bored with the confinement, J.J. headed down the hallway, leaving the marshals to the TV. *Let's see just how good you guys are at your jobs.*

She went back to her bedroom, opened her suitcase, slipped on her running shoes and down vest, then silently opened the window. For a split second she hesitated, hands clenched on the sash, feeling the icy air against her face as she stared out into the unrelieved blackness of the night.

"Dammit." She'd never been afraid before. But just for a nanosecond she'd been terrified of what could be out there in the dark waiting for her.

She never would have pulled a stunt like this in D.C. But this was the back of beyond. Nobody here knew her. And nobody knew where she was. If she wasn't safe here, she wasn't safe anywhere.

Now or never.

She drew in a deep breath and swung her legs through the opening.

It was an easy drop to the ground.

The air was cool and crisp. Snow crunched beneath her feet as she eased the window closed. Bringing her heel up to her butt, she stretched out her hamstring, then repeated the action on the other leg. With only the half-moon as her guide, she began a light jog west. Running had always been a great stress reliever and she certainly needed that now.

She'd gone about a mile and a quarter when she started to feel fatigue.

"Not possible," she panted into the dead quiet of the dark night. She was a marathon-class runner. Had to be the lingering effects of the surgery. Her body never tired this quickly. Maybe it was the altitude. That would explain the fatigue, the nausea and the general "off" feeling.

"Except that I felt off before I left D.C.," she argued with herself. Maybe the doctors missed something. She hadn't exactly been much help. She didn't even remember the beating, so she couldn't give specifics.

Stubbornness kept her moving. Replaced ten minutes later by the sight of streetlights up ahead. Jasper wasn't much more than a dot in the middle of the valley. But on the way to the safe house, she'd seen a diner—the Something-or-Another Café. She'd go inside, have an all night drink, maybe read the local paper. See just how long it would take the crack team of U.S. marshals to realize their protectee was gone.

She smiled, knowing full well her boss would enjoy reading her report. Red was fiercely competitive with any other law enforcement branch. He was old school FBI—in his mind, *they* were the elite. He'd like that J.J. bested the marshals on the very first night. Maybe that could earn her some points, make up for the whole Visnopov debacle.

Feeling a true sense of purpose, J.J. turned right when she hit Main Street and slowed her pace as she passed the metered parking spots and expertly restored buildings. Just past the courthouse, she saw a lot filled with pickup trucks. The Cowboy Café was apparently a hopping place.

J.J. almost gagged when she stepped inside. The smell of bacon and coffee assailed her while about twenty pairs of eyes turned in her direction. An attractive redhead J.J. put somewhere in the vicinity of fifty smiled as she came out from behind a chipped Formica counter. A pencil was stuck behind her ear. Said ear was decorated with snowman earrings that bobbed and swayed with each step she took.

"I'm Ruthie. Want a table or the counter?"

"A booth, please," J.J. answered, following as the

woman led her through the gauntlet of inquiring eyes to the next to last booth.

"Coffee?" Ruthie asked, the pencil now poised above a pad with worn, curled corners.

"Ginger ale?"

Ruthie tilted her head and looked down with unabashed curiosity in her intelligent green eyes. "Tea, if you're feeling the mountains."

Whatever that meant.

Clearly reading her expression, Ruthie smiled. "That's the altitude, honey. Tea and toast," she recommended. "Don't worry, honey. Happens to a lot of visitors. I'll get you fixed up in a jiff. But you shouldn't be out running until your system adjusts. Especially if you're planning on getting any skiing time in tomorrow."

It made sense for Ruthie to assume she was a tourist. And it made just as much sense for J.J. to let the woman keep that assumption. Smiling, she said, "Sounds great. I'll put myself in your capable hands."

"Come on over here, Ruthie old girl. I'll put you in my hands, too," a rough-looking guy called from his perch on a bar stool held together with some duct tape and a lot of hope.

"Go on home to your wife," Ruthie tossed back good-naturedly. "You know I never put my hands where another woman's belong. And leave the nice blonde alone. She's a guest in our fine town, and we don't want her getting the wrong impression."

Apparently Ruthie's word was gospel in the café. J.J. was served in peace and even given a copy of the local weekly to peruse as she nursed the lemony hot tea.

She was working on the second triangle of bland toast when she heard the screech of tires out front.

Dipping the newspaper fractionally, she watched as all four doors of the SUV swung open.

Here it comes, she thought. *I'm not going to react to his anger. See how he likes that!*

With Cody in the lead, the four marshals burst into the restaurant.

The choruses of "Hey, Cody!" seemed lost on the man as he stormed toward her, his dark eyes glistening, hands fisted at his sides.

Careful not to reveal any reaction, J.J. placed her paper on the table and met his hostile gaze with a deceptively calm smile. "Evening, Deputy Landry."

Chapter Three

It took all his powers of reason to keep his temper in check. Furious seemed too tame a description for the emotions churning into a knot in his gut.

Yanking J.J. out of the seat, Cody hurried her from the café, ignoring the curious stares of the patrons and Ruthie alike. Martin held the door while Lara and Denise took up positions at the rear of the SUV as Cody practically tossed J.J. into the passenger's compartment.

She looked as if she might speak. Cody quickly shot her a warning glance. "Do. Not. Open. Your. Mouth."

Like a small child rebelling, J.J. parted her lips, but no sound emerged.

After slamming the door and instructing the team members to get in, Cody slipped behind the wheel and gunned the engine. Tires squealed as he peeled south on Main.

The acrid smell of burned rubber mirrored the fire smoldering in every cell in his body. What in the hell was she thinking?

"I wanted—"

"Do *not* speak." Cody lifted a single finger in J.J.'s direction. He needed to get a better grip on his emotions before he could carry on any sort of conversation with the woman. And he wasn't quite sure how to go about that.

And the answer didn't present itself in the few miles back to the cabin.

He parked but left the engine running. "You guys take a drive."

"But it's freezing and there's nothing around for miles," Martin complained.

"Go back to the café. I'll need about an hour."

"Guess again," J.J. said, opening the door in the process. "I'm going to bed."

Cody was on her in a heartbeat, grabbing her arm, half-guiding, half-dragging her to the front door and then inside the safe house. "From this moment on, Agent Barnes, you don't do anything without my express permission."

J.J. kept up a brave front—quite an accomplishment given the menacing timbre of his voice and his death grip on her arm. So maybe she shouldn't have ventured out on her own. Maybe it was stupid. But she needed to feel in control. She hadn't asked for this assignment. She loathed the idea of investigating Cody and his team. As much as she would have hated him investigating her.

And J.J. had firsthand experience of just how much she hated being investigated. After her cover was blown, Internal Affairs had been on her like lint on a black suit after a visit to a cotton factory.

"Sit," Cody commanded.

J.J. almost fell as she fumbled behind her, searching for a chair. She and Cody locked narrowed gazes and she wasn't about to be the first to blink. Nope. It would only be interpreted as a sign of weakness and she'd gnaw off her own tongue before she'd ever admit that he was a little intimidating. Well, more than a little.

His hands opened and closed, forming fists as he paced the small living room, his strides long and purposeful. Four steps, pivot, four steps. It was methodical and, frankly, irritating. He was acting like the principal to her delinquent student. If he expected her to sit meekly with her hands folded in her lap, he had another thing coming.

"Be pissed. Don't be pissed," she said as she started to stand, "I really don't care. I'm tired and I'm going to bed."

She was half out of the chair when Cody paralyzed her with a single, pointed stare. For several moments, there was nothing but the sound of his breathing and the occasional crackle from the fireplace.

Shoving the coffee table very close to the edge of her chair, he sat on the edge and leaned forward. Countering the move, J.J. sat farther back in the seat, not wanting to give him the satisfaction of sensing her ill ease.

Cody counted to ten. Again. The sum total of his counting was probably somewhere in the tens of thousands at this point. This woman was making him crazy. She was jeopardizing the assignment. Worse yet, she was jeopardizing her life. And his, and the teams, if he let himself think about it. But personal safety was always secondary to the protectee.

Steepling his fingers, he took a calming breath and let it out slowly. Through sheer will, his pulse was normal and he no longer had an overwhelming urge to shake some sense into her.

"You know the rules, Agent Barnes," he began, allowing his eyes to roam over her face. It was a blank canvas. Save for a single flicker of uncertainty in those incredible aqua eyes, she was a master at keeping her feelings in check. Normally he'd have considered that a plus. But he wasn't feeling too normal.

He was noticing the way the firelight reflected against her hair. His eyes followed her fingers as she gripped the zipper on her vest and slowly pulled down, revealing just a hint of her upper body. Well, more than a hint, actually. He shook his head, trying not to allow his focus to shift to someplace it shouldn't go.

"What possessed you to sneak out of your room?"

"I wanted something to drink." Her gaze flickered away before returning to his face. A lie then. "I was told I couldn't have anything until you came back from doing...*whomever* and I didn't feel like waiting."

He had to smile at the indignation in her tone. "Where did you get that idea?"

She made a little sound, one that conveyed mild disgust and moral superiority. "*Personal time?* Do you think I don't know what that means? You're the DIC, Landry. What kind of example are you setting for your team?"

Her righteous indignation was kind of sexy. "Don't worry about my team," he replied easily, fairly sure that his lack of reaction to her little lecture would push one of her many, many buttons.

It did.

J.J. stood and planted her hands on her hips. She glared down at him, and he noted a tiny vein pulsing at her temple. "It isn't worry, Deputy. It's antipathy. You are responsible for this assignment and you don't seem to realize that your actions set the tone around here. If you were more attentive to your responsibilities, your team would have been more attentive, and I wouldn't have been able to slip out the window. Get it?"

He stood, liking the fact that he was probably one of the few men who towered over this woman. Purposefully he crowded her. Moving so close that he could feel her warm breath against his throat and smell the faint scent of soap and something floral on her skin. "I know my responsibilities, Agent Barnes."

"And racing off to...*fornicate* is one of them?"

He tossed back his head and laughed. "Fornicate? Do you have a sideline going as a televangelist?"

Her lips pursed for a moment and her eyes blazed. "I was attempting to keep my description as neutral as possible. But that in no way negates the impropriety of your actions. Your lapse led directly to tonight's incident."

He placed his hands on her shoulders and gently urged her back into the seat. He gave himself bonus points for not urging her into his arms. Every time she got all haughty and official sounding, he was virtually overwhelmed with the urge to kiss her senseless.

When she was seated again, he allowed his palms to linger, to feel the soft strength beneath the layers of fabric. "I wasn't off on a quickie. I went to see my family."

He waited a few seconds for his words to register. Once they did, he dropped his hands and sat across from her.

"Family?"

He smiled. "Tons of it. As a concession to me, this detail was moved to Montana because I needed to be here for a family thing."

Her forehead wrinkled as she seemed to process the new information. "Then why didn't Martin just say that?"

"Because he probably never thought a well-trained FBI agent would be so stupid as to ditch her protective detail."

A faint stain of color appeared on her cheeks and for the very first time, she dipped her head and the challenge was gone from her eyes.

"Then I apologize."

Almost choked on that, huh? "I need to know I have your cooperation in this, J.J. I can't protect you if you're going to run off every time you get the chance."

She raised her eyes to meet his. The twinge of vulnerability he saw there hit him like a slap. "This is hard for me."

"It'd be hard for me, too," he agreed easily. "I sure wouldn't want to be baby-sat even if it was in my best interest. You're a good agent, J.J. This will pass."

There was no humor in the smile she offered. "You're in very small company on that score. I'm not the most popular person with the bureau right now."

"The Visnopov thing?"

She nodded, then brushed away a few wayward

strands of hair. "I was this close——" she pinched her thumb and forefinger together "——to connecting Goran Visnopov to a dozen murders. I almost had the bastard."

"Until your cover was blown."

"Yes."

He'd read the file, but that single syllable had more impact than the hundred-plus-page dossier. "Even more reason to bite the bullet and stay put. I know the inactivity is hard, but you can still put a hurting on them. With your testimony, the U.S. attorney might be able to flip one of the Russians."

She shook her head vehemently. "Russian mobsters are a different animal. They are remorseless, brutal, fearless and consider our prison system a joke. I spent two years living and interacting with these guys, and I don't think the threat of some time behind bars will be enough to turn anyone against the boss."

Placing his hand against her knee, he gave a little squeeze of encouragement. "You never know, J.J."

"I know that the three people who could tie Prestov and Visnopov directly to the murders are dead. All I can do is testify about their RICO activities."

"And your attack."

She shrugged and he thought she might have paled slightly.

"Not really. I don't remember it."

"Can't that change?"

"Maybe. But the doctors weren't hopeful. Something about my subconscious protecting me from a painful event." She rose and walked over to the fire. Taking the poker, she shoved at the logs and embers, sending bright orange sparks up the flue.

"What do you remember?" Cody asked.

"I got a message from one of my contacts to meet her in Little Kiev at four in the morning. I remember getting out of the cab on Second Avenue...." She paused and a sad smile curved her pretty lips. "Funny, but I vividly remember thinking I would stop at the bakery on my way back to my apartment. There's a great bakery on Seventh. Anyway—" she sighed "—I went into the alley as instructed and was there for only a few seconds before I felt my head explode. I saw a couple of silhouettes, lots of stars, then nothing."

"Ambush."

"Big time. The next thing I knew, I was in the recovery room with a nurse explaining what a spleenectomy was to me."

Cody pointed toward her right cheek. "And it looks like you had a heck of a shiner if you still have a bruise after almost two months."

She let out a breath and touched her fingertips to her face. "Yep. The gift that keeps on giving."

Cody felt a rush of primal rage at the mere thought of J.J. being beaten. Partly because his personal code simply didn't include men beating on women. And because it was *this* woman.

He could only imagine what J.J. would think of him feeling so much as an inkling of personal interest in her.

Do I? he wondered. Or, more importantly, *why would I?*

Cody raked his fingers through his hair. It wasn't as though he'd had a positive history with the woman. He wasn't even on her radar. Maybe that was the very reason he was interested. Pretty feeble, he knew. Nothing was quite as pathetic as a man who was interested in a woman *specifically* because she had shown no interest in him.

"Anyway, it's history," J.J. continued. "If you're finished calling me on the carpet, may I go to bed now?"

With me? Sure. "I want your word, J.J. No more antics."

She shrugged her slender shoulders and held up the wrong number of fingers to validate the Girl Scout Pledge. "Swear."

"We need trust here, J.J., mutual trust if this is going to work out."

"You can trust me," she insisted.

"Then get some sleep."

J.J. went to her room and immediately noticed that her window had been nailed shut. From the outside. So much for trust. Still, she smiled. If he'd thought ahead enough to secure the window, he was more competent than she'd initially given him credit.

Competent and cute.

A dangerous combination.

And a definite problem if she was to maintain her objectivity. "Tough to investigate a guy you wouldn't mind seeing naked," she grumbled as she dug into her suitcase for her pj's.

She'd locked the door, so she felt comfortable leaving her gun and cell phone on the bed. After changing into well-worn, flannel drawstring pants and a form-fitting T-shirt decorated with little stars, she pulled her ponytail free of its holder and ran a brush through her hair as she surveyed her surroundings.

The room was stark but homey. The rustic wooden bed was large—a real bonus for a tall woman—and the comforter looked handmade and warm. Definitely a plus, since she could hear the wind picking up outside. Aside from the bed, there was a simple wooden nightstand and a mismatched, five-drawer dresser with an oval mirror hanging above it. The frame around the mirror was painted the same awful crimson as the dresser. Finished brushing her hair, she walked over to her suitcase and felt along the inside until she found the curling iron.

She returned to the bed and shoved her weapon under the pillow, then sat down and spent a few seconds removing parts from their concealed places inside the heating tube. After a couple of adjustments she had constructed a charger, which she connected to the cell phone.

A small icon flashed, indicating she had a message waiting.

Enjoy your run and your tea?

J.J. scoffed, expecting this as much as she resented it. Obviously the FBI was keeping close tabs on her. She tried to guess which one of the café patrons was a plant. One of the men was her shadow, but which one? Given what had happened in the alley in Little Kiev, she should have been grateful that the FBI had her back. However, she knew full well that if Landry or any of the other deputies found the plant, her assignment would be blown. Something she couldn't afford to happen again.

She typed, her fingers flying over the keypad.

Just doing my job.

She sent the message and was a little surprised when she got an instant reply.

Update?

Landry disappeared for several hours tonight, she wrote.

Explanation?

Need to verify. Background information would help.

Local boy. Six brothers. Raised in Jasper.

Local boy? Associate Director Andrews didn't usually speak in such colloquial terms. Must be the time difference.

Prominent family. Financials clean. Service record clean.

Great butt, she thought, amusing herself. But she typed,

Can't be eliminated yet. Too soon. Barnes out.

Sending new contact info. Out.

Her boss was probably being overly cautious, but she programmed the new number into the phone.

Using her discarded sweats, she covered the phone and the charger before crawling into bed. It felt warm and wonderful and she was all too ready to sleep when she reached for the light switch.

The room went black. The wind rattled the window-panes so loudly, she almost missed the sound of the slowly approaching car.

Pressing a button on the side of her watch, she marked the time. Fifty-five minutes since Cody had sent the team members away and now they were returning. "Very punctual," she whispered in the darkness. "Cody has you all well trai—"

Darkness. No headlights!

Her brain registered the danger a split second before semiautomatic gunfire began to perforate the room.

She felt for her gun just as the door splintered open and Cody grabbed her off the bed, rolling her to the floor and covering her with his heavy body.

The *rat-tat-tat* continued. J.J. smelled cordite and felt plaster raining all around her. She couldn't breathe. And she definitely couldn't move. Not with Cody on top of her.

Then there was silence. Eerie, deafening silence as the echoes faded.

"Are you hit?" Cody asked as he crouched above her, running his hands along her head, shoulders and sides.

"N-no," she finally answered when her lungs reinflated.

"Stay down," he commanded as he crawled over to

the window, gun drawn. Slowly he pressed himself against the wall and slid up, checking outside in a series of jerky glances.

"Clear," he shouted, frustrated.

He looked over as she flipped on the light, and she saw his face go incredibly pale.

"You're bleeding."

Chapter Four

"Hang on," Cody instructed, gently sitting her on the bed as he stuffed his weapon in his waistband and withdrew his cell phone. "Get back here now and give me an ETA."

Hunching over, J.J. pressed both hands, *hard,* to the painful cramps in her abdomen. She had no idea where she'd been hit; she couldn't see a wound.

But between the pain and all the blood she'd definitely been hit.

J.J. winced as the cramping got worse. Something internal—maybe a complication from her surgery?

As if sensing her discomfort, Cody eased her against his chest as he made a second call. "Seth, bro, thank God I got you. There's been a shooting at the Carver Hunting Lodge. Send a unit and an ambulance and have Chance meet me at Community."

Cody shoved the phone into his pocket. He shifted and took her by the shoulders, holding her slightly away from him. The compassion and concern in his eyes was touching and unexpected. "I'm going to lay you back. Where's the entrance wound?"

"I don't know—ouch!"

"Take a guess."

"My abdomen."

Very efficiently, Cody laid her back and placed a pillow beneath her knees. The wail of a siren sounded in the distance. She was about to thank Cody when she saw that he was dangling her gun from his index finger. She expected a pretty good reaming. Instead he shrugged his broad shoulders and said, "We'll talk about this later."

"I'm cold."

Cody yanked the blanket from the end of the bed and placed it on top of her. "Hang in there."

Then everything happened in a rush. EMTs rushed in, transferred her to a gurney and whisked her into the waiting ambulance. An oxygen mask was placed on her face and an IV started.

She heard something about "pressure dropping" and then everything seemed to get fuzzy and confusing.

CODY FELT RELIEF wash over him when his brother, Chance, emerged from the O.R., shoving the blue cloth hat from his head before tugging the mask from his face. Chance appeared tired, but the look he gave him told Cody that everything was fine.

"She'll be in recovery in a few minutes."

Cody rose from the uncomfortable plastic seat. "I heard the nurses say it wasn't a gunshot wound. So, it was the spleen thing, right?"

Chance narrowed his gaze. "I can't give you confidential medical information."

"She's my protectee," Cody argued, falling into step

with his older brother who began walking down the nearly deserted hospital corridor.

"And she's my patient. I'm not going to tell you anything, so stop begging. It isn't manly."

Cody gave Chance a gentle but effective shove with his shoulder. His brother careened off the tiled wall.

"Real adult," Chance scoffed. "You look like hell, Cody. Why don't you go home and get some sleep."

"I can't leave J.J. unguarded."

"Aren't there three other marshals on this thing?" Chance opened the door to the doctors' lounge and invited him inside.

He poured coffee that was thick but obviously hot and Cody was all too happy to accept. Chance fell into one of three large leather chairs and let out an exhausted breath. His neck cracked as he rolled his head around on his shoulders.

Cody tasted the coffee that was as bitter as it smelled. He sat opposite his brother and saw Chance's concerned look at his hastily bandaged hand. "No biggie. I must've cut it when I was crawling through the bedroom. Don't get your stethoscope in a knot. I don't need anything more than a dab of antiseptic and a bandage."

Chance leaned forward and grabbed his hand, unrolling the wad of gauze Cody had applied to the cut. "It needs irrigation and a fresh dressing."

Cody rolled his eyes as he snatched his hand away. "Thanks for the hundred-dollar words, but you're only telling me what I already know—clean it and cover it."

Smiling, Chance went over to a cabinet, grabbed a few first-aid items and tossed them to Cody. "So, what's the deal with the tall, leggy blonde with the spleenectomy scar?"

"Protectee," Cody grumbled.

"Got that part," he retorted, falling back into the chair as he rubbed his face. "I mean, what's her deal?"

Cody finished bandaging his cut and tossed the trash into the can. "Three points."

"Two points," Chance corrected. "You only get three if you hit the can from the sofa. Hospital rules. You were going to tell me about your protectee."

"She's an important cog in an investigation of the Russian mob in New York."

Chance's dark head bobbed. "A mob moll. I think that's a first for me."

"Not a moll," Cody corrected. "Though I probably shouldn't be telling you all this. How about we do a tit for tat. I'll tell you why J.J.'s in protective custody and you tell me what the hell happened to her."

"It's her place to tell you," Chance deflected. "I can get in serious trouble if I betray a medical confidence."

"C'mon, Chance. I'm your brother. Doesn't that count for something?"

"It counts for a lot. But it doesn't mean I'm going to spoon-feed you privileged information on a patient. So, get over it. You're starting to whine like Shane."

"Nobody can whine like Shane," Cody joked. "Okay, since we have this impasse, let's change the subject. How's life been treating you?"

"I love being a dad," he answered without a second of hesitation. "And I can't wait for you to meet Chloe. She's the most beautiful baby in the history of the Landry clan."

"Thanks to Val," Cody remarked, knowing full well Chance would launch the empty cup at his head. He did. But missed. "Losing your skills in your old age, I see."

"I haven't lost anything," Chance insisted, lingering sibling rivalry dripping from every syllable. "I'm just tired because my brother called me out of my warm bed for an emergency."

"That's your job," Cody remarked without remorse. "You're the one who chose medicine. You knew the hours when you signed on."

"Speaking of hours, why don't you try to grab a nap? During my residency I learned to sleep whenever I could for however long I could."

Pressing his palms against his knees, Cody hoisted himself out of the chair. "I've got things to do. First and foremost, I've got to find another safe house. The Carver place looks a lot like Bonnie and Clyde's car."

"Seth said it was bad. Have you talked to him yet?"

"Nope. I'll put that on my list."

"Here's something else for your list," Chance said, putting a fraternal arm on Cody's shoulder. "Cut J.J. some slack for a while. She's been through hell."

"What does that mean?"

Chance didn't answer.

"Which way to recovery?"

"I'll show you." Chance had taken two steps when he stopped short and turned back to glare at Cody.

"What?"

"I'm not kidding. I don't care what this woman did or is going to do, but right here, right now, she's my patient. I don't want you to do anything to—"

Cody groaned. "Get over yourself. I've heard everything you've said. I'll be on my best behavior, but I *will* find out what happened."

"Let her tell you in her own time."

Cody scratched his head. What could she need time to tell? He knew all about the beating—more than J.J. knew herself. He'd seen the medical reports. Maybe she'd remembered a detail. That would be pretty traumatic and would explain Chance's odd behavior.

"THIS IS UNACCEPTABLE, Miss Barnes," the harried little nurse was saying as she helped J.J. into a drab green pair of surgical scrubs. "Dr. Landry left specific instructions that you needed rest. You're to be admitted for the night."

"Change in plans," she told the woman, holding out her hand so the IV could be removed. Stubbornly the woman crossed her arms in front of her and glared. "Your call," J.J. commented, reaching for the pressure bandage on the nearby instrument cart.

"You can't take that out."

"Oh…but I can," J.J. countered. And she would have if Cody and his brother hadn't appeared in the recovery area at that instant.

Uh-oh. Busted.

"What are you doing?" they asked in unison. Equal parts surprise and disapproval.

She was unfazed and directed her gaze to Cody. "I'm getting out of this very public place."

"Not necessary," Cody argued. "Denise, Lara and Martin are coordinating with the local authorities. All the entrances and exits are covered. All visitors will be screened before—"

"This is a community hospital, right?"

Chance nodded.

"I'm not willing to compromise the care or security of the community after what happened tonight. The faster I get out of here, the safer everyone will be."

Cody stepped forward. "I can keep you safe here, J.J."

"Just like at the Carver place?" she tossed back. "You may be able to keep me safe, but what about all the other people here? Is it worth the risk of some civilian getting caught in the cross fire?"

Cody's mouth pulled into a tight line, then he turned to his brother. "Is it safe for her to travel?"

"I wouldn't recommend it."

"But is it safe?" Cody pressed.

"Not far," Chance relented. "There could still be complications."

"Any suggestions?"

Chance stroked his chin, then suggested, "Dora Simms' place is empty. I can call her brother and—"

"No calls," Cody insisted. "At least not from you or anyone else connected to the family. I'll handle that. You get her ready to travel."

Cody disappeared through the shiny double doors, leaving J.J. with Chance and the nurse. Not for long, though. The nurse was dismissed, and not, judging by her reaction, all too keen on the idea.

Chance went about removing the IV so slowly and methodically, J.J. almost shoved aside his hand and did it herself.

"I don't think this is a good idea," he said.

"Due respect, Doctor, I don't really give a fig. I'm not going to be responsible for anyone else getting harmed. In case you didn't hear the news, I've got some very, very bad people who want me very, very dead."

"Which could happen anyway if you start hemorrhaging again."

"Are all Landrys such soothsayers of doom?"

Chance smiled and J.J. found herself comparing it to Cody's. A close second, at best.

"We're a pretty positive group and we do protect our own," Chance told her with confidence.

"I'm hardly one of yours. I'm Cody's assignment. Period." *And possibly his worst enemy.* She'd been running through the evening's events in her mind. Cody had made the call to send the team members away from the safe house. Had he put her in a vulnerable position because he was Visnopov's leak?

But if that was true, why had he rushed into the hail of bullets?

"I'm putting together a care package for you," Chance explained. He held out a plastic sack with the hospital's logo on it. Once she accepted it, he held out his card and dropped it inside. "I want to hear from you at least twice a day. If I don't, I'll come and find you."

"That won't be necessary," she insisted, gently getting down from the gurney to stand on unsure footing. "I'm perfectly capable of handling myself."

"I don't doubt that," Chance remarked.

She looked up and silently thanked him for his sincerity and his care.

"But that doesn't mean you have to keep all this bottled inside of you. J.J., you need—"

"To handle this my own way. Really—" she patted his forearm "—I'm fine. No big deal." She ran her fingers through her hair and planted a perfect smile on her face. "I'll keep in touch."

"Twice a day."

IT WAS ONLY because of his promise to Chance that he'd agreed to return to the Carver place a few minutes later so J.J. could pack her own bag. He'd sent the rest of the team ahead to secure the old Simms farm.

They arrived at the hunting lodge amid a throng of activity. Seth was waiting on the front porch as Cody placed the SUV in Park.

"Another Landry?" J.J. asked.

"We're everywhere," he joked. "You can't walk ten feet in Jasper without tripping over one of us."

"A marshal, a doctor and now a sheriff? Are you all a bunch of adrenaline junkies?"

He shot her a grin. "All but Shane. He's the baby and the family slacker."

She laughed softly.

He liked the sound. A lot. "Someday, when we're on our hundredth game of gin rummy, I'll give you the whole family tree. For now, let's get you packed."

Cody didn't have both feet on the ground when he was caught in his brother's slapping embrace.

"Nothing like making your presence known," Seth teased. "It's great to see you."

"You, too. Meet Agent J.J. Barnes," Cody said as J.J. rounded the car.

"A true pleasure, Agent Barnes."

The two shook hands. It all seemed cordial enough, but Cody noted that J.J. still didn't look right. Dammit! He never should have agreed to let her leave the hospital.

"He's a flirt," Cody cut in, taking J.J.'s elbow and leading her through the collection of officers and into the lodge. "He has a beautiful wife at home and he still flirts. It's shameful."

"Are you the only holdout?"

"Marriagewise? Nope. Shane and I are the bachelors. Chandler turns in his dating card in less than two weeks."

"There're too many of you. My head is spinning trying to remember everyone. By the way, did your mother and father have a perverse thing for 'C' and 'S' names?"

"Let's see…Cody, Chandler, Chance, Clayton, Sam, Seth, Shane.

"Yep." But he didn't want to discuss his parents. A quick pack and run. That was the goal. "I'll give you a hand."

"No!" she insisted.

Vehemently enough that it caught his attention. Turning to look at her hooded eyes, he wondered what was going on in that complicated brain of hers. "I'm pretty sure Chance said no heavy lifting for a week to ten days."

"I won't lift. I'd just like a few minutes to organize my stuff."

"We don't have a lot of time."

"Please? I just want a few minutes to myself."

One look at her big, solemn eyes and he caved. Completely, totally, instantly caved. "Fine. I'll wait here."

Slowly she crossed the living room. He watched her gingerly steps with compassion and concern. "J.J.?"

"Yes?" she responded, turning back toward him.

"Get your stuff together, then call me. I'll carry it out to the truck."

"Thanks." She turned back toward the door.

He paced for the full three minutes it took her to pack her suitcase and call for him. Walking back into her bedroom was a vile reminder of the evening's events. The room was freezing because there were so many holes shot through the walls. The window was shattered, and plaster had left a layer of white dust on nearly everything. It was a wonder they hadn't both been killed.

"It just needs to be zipped," she said, pointing to the suitcase as she pulled on her vest.

"You're lucky," Seth commented as he entered the room. "Cody usually shirks all menial tasks."

"Don't you have some speeding tickets to write?" Cody tossed back as he lifted the suitcase onto its wheels.

"Not for another hour," Seth joked, winking at J.J. "We've pulled one hundred and seventeen slugs from the walls so far. I'm sending them to the lab in Helena."

"I want the forensics as soon as they're available," Cody replied. "Can I still commandeer a few of your men?"

"Already done. The road to Dora's is sealed up tight."

"Thanks," Cody said with feeling. "I want to get her there and in bed ASAP. I'll be in touch."

"Don't forget dinner," Seth called as they were leaving the cabin.

"I may not make it. Tell Molly to send me a memo on my duties and responsibilities."

"She won't take no for an answer," Seth responded from the porch. "She's determined to have every Landry present and involved in this wedding."

"And I'm determined not to let my protectee get killed." Cody realized a little too late that he probably shouldn't have said that in front of J.J.

SMALL TALK wasn't her forte, J.J. thought as they were once again alone, driving toward the new safe house. Especially not when she was weak, tired, feeling pretty lousy and confused as all get-out. Seeing the way Cody interacted with his family simply didn't fit the profile of someone leaking information to the Russian mob. What would he gain?

She knew his family was loaded, so it couldn't be about the money. He did seem willing to bend the rules a bit. Which had worked to her advantage. She had retrieved her cell phone and packed away the charger without him ever guessing.

Maybe the Visnopovs had something on him.

She glanced over at his profile and was surprised to see deep lines etched by his eyes. His lips were pulled taut and he seemed...distracted? Pensive? What?

"Something wrong?" she asked.

"Guilt."

Because you ratted me out to the Visnopovs? "Over?"

He flipped down the visor, cutting the glare from the morning sun reflecting off the pristine snow. "You."

"Care to expand on that?"

"Depends on you."

She noted that his grip tightened on the steering wheel.

"What happened, J.J.?"

"We got shot at?"

"Not that," he said, clearly exasperated. "Did I hurt you?"

"Hurt me?" she parroted, not following at all.

"I fell on you pretty hard. Is that what caused the bleeding? Is that why Chance wouldn't tell me anything?"

"No. One thing has nothing to do with the other."

"I don't believe you," he insisted. "I've been racking my brain and it's the only scenario that makes sense. I know you pride yourself on being tough. You had to be. Hell, no one has ever been able to penetrate the Visnopov organization except you. That's an impressive accomplishment. I respect that."

"Thanks."

"I can't stand knowing that I hurt you. That's not the way I do things."

"I'm sure."

"So tell me what I did."

"You didn't do anything," she insisted. "It was just an unavoidable…*thing*. I'm fine. I'll be fine. Put it out of your mind."

"Hard to let go of something you don't understand. Like the gun. Or did you think I'd give you a pass on carrying a weapon?"

"I'm a federal agent, Cody. I carry a weapon at all times."

"Not when you're under my supervision." His actions belied his words when he reached across her, retrieved her gun from the glove compartment and placed it in her lap. "You shouldn't have hidden it, J.J. I have no problem with you keeping your weapon."

Why did he have to be so nice? It was just what she didn't need when her emotions were so jumbled. For the first time since Brian Gellman had dumped her in high school, she was on the verge of public tears.

"What?" Cody demanded, apparently sensing her fragility. "What is it, J.J.? What aren't you telling me?"

"Drop…it." Her voice caught on each syllable.

Cody wasted no time veering the car onto the shoulder of the road, then bringing the vehicle to a sudden stop. Unhooking his shoulder belt, he turned in the seat as much as he was able. One hand reached out and he hooked a finger beneath her chin, forcing her to meet his gaze.

His expression was a jigsaw of emotions—curiosity, concern, guilt. She felt the warm track of a tear as it spilled onto her cheek. Cody's thumb moved up to wipe it away.

"Please, J.J., talk to me."

"I can't."

"You can," he insisted, punctuating the statement with a weak smile. "I'm tough. Tell me what I did. How did I hurt you?"

"You didn't," she insisted, feeling her eyes well with new tears. "I don't even know why I'm crying. It isn't like I should feel sad."

"About?" he pressed.

"I mean, I should be relieved. It wasn't something I planned."

She watched as recognition dawned.

"The blood. You miscarried. You were pregnant and you didn't bother to tell anyone?" He sat back, raking his fingers through his hair, then rubbed his face. "That was stupid. You should have said something. We would have…"

He stopped speaking. She knew exactly what he was thinking even before he turned damning brown eyes on her.

Chapter Five

"Don't you dare give me that *look*," J.J. told him, chin thrust out, shoulders squared. "This is none of your business and not open for discussion."

"The hell it isn't," Cody returned with equal force. "I've gone out of my way to treat you in the same fashion I'd treat a male protectee." He paused, rubbing his face. "Jeez, J.J., I've been yanking you around, something I would not have done had I known you were pregnant. I saw you on the obstacle course at Quantico. You are—*were*—more fit than most guys I know."

"Get over it, Landry. No one is blaming you."

"I am," he told her, those chocolate eyes filling with open, raw guilt. "How am I supposed to look you in the face knowing I caused your miscarriage? Didn't your doctor—"

"*You* didn't cause anything, and I never saw a doctor."

He grew quiet again and she could almost hear his brain zipping through all the possibilities. He must have settled on one, because the guilt she'd seen in his eyes melded into something harsh and unyielding. "Why didn't you see a doctor, Barnes? You're smarter than that. You had surgery and follow-ups, so it wasn't like you didn't have time or access to prenatal care."

"What are you, a public service announcement?" she snapped, exasperated and embarrassed. "I'm not discussing my health with you, Landry."

"Why not?" he insisted.

His voice was deceptively calm and quiet. It was more intimidating than listening to him bluster. She shrugged and turned toward the window, needing to get out from under his probing eyes.

Cody's fingers hooked her chin, applying pressure until she finally relented and turned her head to look at him.

"Why not? Why didn't you see a doctor? Why didn't you tell anyone? Don't shrug or tell me you don't know. Those are toddler answers."

Shoving his hand off her, J.J. said nothing, her stomach churning. She was a bundle of emotion—not something she was accustomed to. She felt splayed open and out of control. *Again with the tears?* she mutely wondered. Her eyes stung, but she was able to stave off the powerful urge to cry.

Of course Cody wasn't helping. She felt like a suspect in a film noir, Cody's unrelenting gaze more disconcerting than a spotlight. "Well, I *don't* know."

Moving back so that he rested half against the door, he regarded her for a long moment. A muscle twitched in his cheek. "I do."

"Really?" She let sarcasm punctuate the single word. "You can't know anything, Landry. You don't know me."

The smile on his face was completely lacking humor. "I *do* know you, Barnes—at least I know your type."

"I don't have a *type*."

"Sure you do. You're so bent on proving you're as good as any man on the job that you'll do whatever it takes to get it done. Including sleeping with the enemy." He let out a nasty-sounding little laugh. "Here I was impressed as sh-*sin* that you managed to infiltrate the Visnopovs and it never dawned on me that you slept your way in."

Her eyes grew wide at the ugly accusation. The sucker punch literally made her heart pause. Her mouth went dry as she stared at his face. He was absolutely serious. "Are you out of your mi—"

"Save it," he cut in, derision in his tone. "I'm just amazed that you were stupid enough not to use protection."

Shock and indignation quickly and fiercely evolved into anger. Hot, fiery never-this-pissed-before anger. "You would have used protection, right?"

"Damned right," he said as he shifted back behind the wheel and gripped the gearshift.

"You hypocritical bastard. You've probably slept with someone to further a case or your career—or whatever the reason—but because you probably used a condom, that gives you the right to be all smug and superior with me?"

"Pretty much…yes."

She spent a few minutes glaring at him before saying, "You're a bigger ass than I thought."

"I don't think you're in any position to be name-calling, Barnes."

Sexist jerk. She folded her hands in her lap and focused her eyes straight ahead. Her heart had started beating again after the accusation, but it felt sluggish and heavy in her tight chest. "The only mistake I made on the Visnopov investigation," she said through her teeth, "was underestimating the danger of the situation."

"You think? Look, I'm sorry you were hurt. But no wonder Visnopov had his goons beat the crap out of you. He must've been pretty ripped when he realized his bed buddy was an FBI plant."

"I'm only going to say this once," J.J. said tightly. "I did *not* sleep with anyone even remotely connected to the Visnopov organization."

Though he was in her peripheral vision, she chose not to look. It was annoying enough to hear his breathing, sense his overwhelming presence and catch the faint scent of his cologne in the tight confines of the car. Right now she hated Cody Landry more than she'd ever hated anyone in her life. She didn't care how the situation looked. For reasons she couldn't quite grasp right now, she was devastated that he'd believe the worst of her. Why that should hurt this badly, she had no idea. It just did. Call it hormones, call it insanity. His erroneous accusation went straight to her heart.

Double jerk. "Drive. It's broad daylight. We're sitting here on the side of the road practically begging to be targets."

"Boyfriend?"

He was like a dog with a bone, and his reasonable tone sent her annoyance up another notch. She didn't like the fact that when he wasn't being an ill-informed, confrontational jackass, she found his voice soothing. Go figure. She was losing what was left of her mind.

"Haven't had a lot of time for that of late." She kept her own tone even, then turned her head to look at him. "Why? Are you going to tell me how pointless it is to try to have a relationship in our line of work? Or how unfair it is to a significant other given the dangerous situations we're in day in and day out? Tell me something I don't know."

"If it wasn't a boyfriend…then someone raped you? Who? When?"

She dropped her head and stared at her hands. She wasn't sure which was worse, his original accusation, or his sympathy. "I can answer two out of three." She struggled to speak over the lump lodged in her throat. "The night I was beaten…the rape kit was positive."

He cursed and the whole car shook when he smashed his open palms against the steering wheel. "Why in the hell didn't—"

"Stop yelling at me!" She was horrified to feel tears rolling down her cheeks to drip into her lap. "By the time I regained consciousness, the doctor told me it was too late for a morning after pill. By the time I left the hospital, I had convinced myself that it couldn't have happened. I mean, who doesn't remember being raped?"

"But your boss—"

"Doesn't know," she said as she impatiently scrubbed away the tears with the back of her hands. "I begged the doctors not to release that part. I knew how it would look."

"Yeah, like the Visnopovs are rapist pigs."

"No," she corrected, slowly turning to look into his eyes. She saw anger and something else she couldn't define. "If anyone knew, I'd be labeled forever. I sure wouldn't be sent back out into the field. I'd spend the rest of my career behind a desk."

"But once you knew you were pregnant—"

"*Suspected,*" she conceded. "I found lots of creative ways to deny the possibility. I chalked every symptom up to the surgery. It was easier than facing the truth."

"You could have told me. You *should've,*" he insisted as he wiped away a stray tear with his thumb.

Pulling away from his touch, she offered a weak smile. "Don't be nice to me right now, Landry. I'm feeling weird and I need to work through that."

"What you need," he began, shoving the armrest aside to move closer, "is this."

He flicked off her seat belt and folded her against him. Tucking the top of her head beneath his chin, Cody laced his fingers through her hair, while, with his other hand, he gently stroked her back. It took a few minutes before he heard the pitiful sounds of her sobs racking her body.

How long—if ever—had it been since she'd let go? How hard had it been to keep all this bottled up inside for what? Almost two months? He couldn't imagine. Being one of seven, he was never at a loss for a confidant.

However, he wasn't stubborn J.J. Barnes who thought anything less than absolute competence was a sign of weakness. It was probably killing her to be held and comforted, but he didn't care. She needed it.

It was some time before he felt her move. Felt her begin to pull out of his embrace. Reluctantly he let her go.

"Better?"

She smiled weakly. "Not really. No."

"I can hold you some more."

Her smile broadened. "Using you as a crutch is a great way to solve my problems."

Shrugging as he slipped back into his seat, he said, "I'm available."

"This from the guy who just reamed me when he thought I was...*involved* during a case?"

Cody's gut tensed as he recalled his harsh words. "I'm really sorry about—"

Raising her hand, she cut him off. "Don't apologize. Just promise me that you won't say anything to anyone."

"It should be part of the investigation, J.J. The U.S. Attorney can charge the—"

Vehemently, she shook her head. "No. I'd like to come out of this with my career intact. The Visnopovs are guilty of enough other crimes to put them out of business forever." She offered him a pretty smile that reached all the way to her incredible eyes. "The Visnopovs can't hurt me anymore. How could they? I've got you around for protection, so what could possibly happen?"

Guilt surged through him. *You can find out I'm supposed to use you as bait.*

SEVEN DAYS into her recovery, J.J. was climbing the walls—*or at least she planned to.* There were no lingering effects from the miscarriage, but the physical inactivity was a problem on two fronts. For a woman used to daily runs of anywhere from five to ten miles, lying around made her muscles feel like mush. More distressing was that she had *way* too much time to think. Well, that ended right now.

The marshals—along with the local authorities, which pretty much meant brother Seth—had sealed the Simms farm off from the rest of the world. Had it not been for her ability to secretly send text messages, J.J. would have been cut off cold. Strangely the several-times-a-day messages had become informal and frankly, odd. She just couldn't reconcile the chatty e-mails with her gruff, no-nonsense boss. His writing seemed almost…friendly and he apparently had a sense of humor that occasionally came out in the communiqués.

"Where are you going?" Lara asked, looking up from the newspaper and sizing up J.J.'s outdoor gear as she entered the small, tidy kitchen.

Grabbing a mug from a cup tree on the dated Formica counter, J.J. poured herself a cup of coffee and joined the deputy marshal at the round oak table that was the focal point of the room. "Good morning to you, too," she greeted.

"Sorry," Lara grumbled.

J.J. figured the boredom was probably getting to Lara as well. How many crossword puzzles could a person do before she started to get itchy?

"I'm heading to the barn," J.J. said after sipping the strong coffee. Too strong, which she knew meant Denise had made this pot. From her surveillance she had learned some specifics about her detail. Aside from making tarlike coffee, Denise had the heart *un*healthy habit of skipping breakfast, preferring to snack on choc-olate bars throughout the day.

Martin was the predictable one. He could usually be found in front of the old television set. J.J. figured he probably had a callus on his thumb from abusing the remote control.

Her current companion was pretty high-strung, with a penchant for minimalist conversation. J.J. hadn't yet figured out why Lara intentionally distanced herself from the rest of the team. Maybe she just didn't feel comfortable with the group. After all, she was the newest member.

Or the leak.

"I need some exercise," J.J. said, running her fingernail along the rim of the mug. "Laziness begets laziness."

Lara smiled. It seemed a reluctant expression, as if Lara hadn't done it enough over the course of her lifetime.

"Cody said you were supposed to take it easy."

"I'm sure Cody says a lot of things," J.J. returned, offering a conspiratorial look that Lara seemed to enjoy. "I feel fine. It's a beautiful day."

Lara scoffed and glanced out the small window above the sink. "If you like the tundra."

"It's refreshingly...*crisp* outside."

"I'm from Alabama," Lara countered. "Anything below fifty degrees is flat-out cold."

"You don't have much of an accent," J.J. commented, hoping to sound conversational since this was the first detail she'd actually culled from Lara.

Lara shrugged her shoulders. "I moved away when I was a teenager. I'm not small town material."

"How small?"

"Less than five hundred nosy, opinionated, self-righteous people. I don't miss it."

Serious hostility there. J.J. made a note to have her boss dig into it. Could be nothing more than a genuine dislike of her hometown, but J.J.'s gut was telling her it might just be important.

"Do you have family in Alabama?"

Lara nodded. "I'm related to about a dozen of said self-righteous folks."

J.J. rose to dump the remnants of the coffee into the sink, then began to stretch out her hamstrings. "The exterior of the barn makes a perfect climbing wall."

Lara groaned. "The perfect climbing wall is in a gym. Cut me some slack, Barnes. Cody will ream me if I let you leave the house. And even if he never knows about it, I have zero desire to stand out in the cold."

"You don't have to. You can see me just fine from here. By the way, where is Landry?" J.J. hoped the question sounded more casual than it felt. She *really* wanted to know why she'd barely seen him for the better part of a week even though they were staying in the same house. *Why is he avoiding me?* Something she didn't dare ask aloud.

"Gone when I got up," Lara said. "Probably more family stuff. From the bits and pieces I've gotten, it sounds like this wedding is the social event of the season." She folded the paper and placed it on the table. She stood up, scraping the chair legs across the rutted linoleum in the process. "I'll get my coat."

"No," J.J. insisted. "Stay inside. If the Visnopovs knew my location, they'd have made a move before now. I'll be fifty yards away and your line of sight is un-obstructed." J.J. led Lara to the window and pointed out at the white landscape.

"Look out there. There aren't any unaccounted-for tracks in the snow, and no way anyone could approach the house or the barn without leaving an obvious trail." She sensed Lara was vacillating, so she continued. "There's not enough of a tree line to provide sniper cover, not that the Visnopovs would ever use a sniper. They like public and bloody. Seriously, Lara, hang out here where it's warm."

"Nowhere but the barn?"

J.J. crossed her heart. "Promise."

"Why do I think this will come back to bite me?" Lara said on a sigh. "Go ahead."

Not wanting to risk Lara suffering a change of heart, J.J. fairly ran out the door. Snow crunched beneath her boots as she first walked, then jogged toward the four-story barn. The air tasted clean and fresh as she sucked in deep breaths.

The sun felt warm against her back as she reached her target. The horizontal wooden boards had just enough space for her to get a decent footing, so she began to climb. Mindful that she didn't want to overexert herself, J.J. kept her pace slow and easy. Gloves would have been a good idea. The weathered wood was dry and splinters tried to attack her palms each time she hoisted herself higher.

Stale air from inside the barn wafted out between the slats. Since this was her first barn, she hadn't expected it to be so large. Peeking inside, she counted no fewer than twenty-five empty stalls. It was hard to see much farther inside since the only light source was slashes of sunlight that seemed to create more shadows than anything else.

Then she saw movement. She froze and strained to bring the image into focus. The outline of a man? Definitely. Martin? No. Cody. Definitely Cody. She knew those shoulders. She'd seen them in her dreams enough times to recognize them even in the worst possible lighting conditions.

So what was he doing in a deserted barn?

Talking to himself?

No. Talking on his cell phone. The words were faint and garbled. Damn! Placing her cheek against the space between the boards, she concentrated to hear the fragments of the one-sided conversation.

"…you have to get her *here!* Time is running out."

Her heart pounded in her ears as she processed the snippet she'd overheard. Was there a positive way to interpret his comments?

No!

Scurrying down the wall, she dashed back toward the house, trying to figure out her next move.

Get concrete confirmation that Cody was the leak before she said anything to her superiors.

How?

Confront him straight-out and get him to confess.

How?

Winded, J.J. ran into the house, claimed an urgent bathroom need to a clearly startled Lara and Denise, and dashed up the stairs. Her original intent had been to get to her room so she could calmly and carefully consider her options. That intent changed when she saw the door to Cody's assigned room ajar.

The temptation was just too great.

Normally the door was closed and, normally, she wouldn't risk violating his space with two of the marshals in the kitchen. But she wasn't feeling all too normal.

Easing inside, she silently closed the door and took two deep breaths in order to halt her racing heart. Her eyes darted around the room. The bed was neatly made. Nothing on the top of the dresser or night table.

"Did you think he'd leave a To Do list sitting out?" she grumbled.

Seeing no other option, she began a careful search of the room. Especially careful, when she realized that Cody Landry was a certifiable neat freak. Everything was precisely folded and organized.

The top dresser drawer held socks rolled into perfect balls. She squeezed them to see if he might have hidden something inside. Nothing. The next drawer contained a neat row of T-shirts and boxer shorts. Nothing out of the ordinary. Unless she acknowledged that her mental image of him standing in front of her wearing nothing except said boxer shorts was abnormal.

She moved on to the other drawers. And again found nothing of interest. She felt under the sheets, inside the pillowcases and between the mattresses. Still nothing.

Placing her hands on her hips, she surveyed the room for someplace—*anyplace*—he might use to hide incriminating materials. The house was more than a hundred years old, so instead of a closet, a wardrobe stood in one corner. The interior was as it should be—a precise row of shirts and slacks hanging from a metal rod. A stack of three blankets was at the bottom, as well as two pairs of shoes. Nothing in the shoes or blankets. J.J. even went so far as to separate the clothing to feel along the rear of the wardrobe for a false back. Nada.

Defeated and frustrated, she turned to leave when she caught a reflection in the nearby window. A flash really. Of something white taped to the wardrobe.

Peering around the furniture, she reached for the piece of paper. Three words were printed on the worn business card: Wilkofski and Associates.

Could be Russian. "No phone number?" she whispered aloud.

Flipping it over, she found a notation written in a bold hand. It was a date—October tenth.

The blood stilled in her veins.

The day she was attacked.

Chapter Six

Cody cursed loudly, then cursed again.

His morning wasn't working out too well and it didn't look like improvement was on the menu as he drove the distance between the Simms farm and the Lucky 7.

The long driveway leading up to the ranch house had been plowed, so the going was pretty easy. His mood was not. He could think of about ten things he'd rather be doing than reviewing—for the umpteenth time—the Chandler-Molly Wedding Extravaganza Checklist. He doubted if a State Visit required this much preplanning or coordination.

His brothers were wrong. It wasn't Molly who was so insistent that every detail be planned, reviewed, adjusted and replanned before finalization. Nope, that was vintage Chandler. Cody knew that from sharing a room with the guy for fifteen long, argument-filled years.

Okay, so living with Chandler had taught him the importance of keeping things neat. In the long run, those habits had made his life less complicated. He could pack in a moment's notice, and his organization had helped him move up in the ranks at work. But he certainly didn't take it to the extreme his alphabetizing, color-coding brother lived by. Poor Molly. And she seemed like such a sensible woman.

His brother's pretty fiancé was waiting for him on the porch holding a very sensible clipboard. Oh-oh. *Doesn't bode well for me.*

Sighing, Cody parked between Seth's Jeep and Sam's Jaguar.

Because it was the first time in more than six years that all the Landrys would be together to celebrate a wedding, Cody knew it was important that he go with the flow. Only problem was, his mind kept drifting back to the Simms farm and his responsibilities there. Or— more honestly—J.J. Barnes.

The wedding was three days away, which meant he had seventy-two more hours of juggling family responsibilities and his job.

"Hi, there," Molly greeted cheerfully, balancing on tiptoe to place a kiss on his cheek. "Thanks for meeting us here so early."

Early? Hardly. "Not a problem. Is everyone here?"

His question didn't really require an answer. Not when he could hear all the noise coming from inside the house. He smiled in spite of his distracted thoughts. This was like old times. Very old times. When seven unruly boys dominated every waking hour in this house.

He had one foot in the door when Kevin, the second oldest of the new generation of Landrys, rushed past on his way into the living room, with no fewer than four of his cousins—some barely able to run—in hot pursuit.

Bringing up the rear was Jessica, Cody's cousin Cade's daughter from his first marriage. Jess had grown into a stunning twenty-two-year-old who apparently was assigned the exhausting task of corralling the young ones while the final wedding plans were hashed out. *For the last time, I hope.*

"Hey, Cody!" Jess yelled, shifting an infant to her right hip as she tried, vainly, to keep pace with her unruly charges.

"Let 'em know who's in charge!" Molly called after her.

"I will as soon as I know!"

"Too many doughnuts," Molly explained as she led him into the den.

It was crowded. Seth was sitting in the leather chair next to the fireplace with his wife, Savannah, balanced on the arm at his side. Chance and Val had grabbed pillows and were lounging on the floor with baby Chloe tucked between them. Very pregnant Tory sat propped at one end of the sofa with Clayton rubbing the small of her back. Sam was sitting at the other end of the sofa, his wife, Callie on his lap. Shane was sprawled in the center of the floor, head propped on Chance's leg. He looked comfortable until Taylor managed to "accidentally" kick him as she made the rounds with a carafe of fresh coffee.

"Hey!" Shane grumbled the third time Taylor's tennis shoe made contact with his thigh.

"Don't like it?" she challenged sweetly, "then get out of my way."

"I have a better idea," Shane retorted as he eased into a sitting position. "Why don't you g—"

"Stop this," Molly chided as she went to stand next to Chandler, who held a stack of file folders. Cody almost groaned aloud. And judging from the looks on the faces of his siblings, he knew they shared his feelings.

"It's still not too late," Clayton offered. "You could fly to Vegas, get married and be home by dinnertime."

Molly paused and Chandler shot Clayton a look that everyone assembled recognized as a warning.

"Ignore them," Callie piped up. "Men have so little appreciation when it comes to the importance of properly planning a wedding."

"I appreciate that it shouldn't take more strategy sessions than planning the invasion of a small country. Ouch!" Shane rubbed his bicep where Taylor had delivered a pretty decent punch considering she was little more than a wisp of a woman. "That's going to leave a bruise."

"Sneeze hard and you bruise, wuss-boy," Sam commented. "I've got a meeting with a client in two hours, so can we get this started, please?"

"Okay," Molly began, taking a pencil from behind her ear. "Taylor, as my maid of honor, you'll—"

When Cody's cell phone chimed, every eye in the room glared in his direction. "Sorry," he muttered, "but I *am* working right now." Hurriedly he retreated into the hallway.

Part of him was relieved by the reprieve the incoming call had given him. Depressing the button to call up the text message, he felt a small smile curve his lips. It faded when he read the message.

Request immediate info on Wilkofski and Associates. Barnes out.

"Well, well, Little Miss Honest To A Fault J.J. You've been snooping around, have you?" He contemplated answering her as he had been doing for days.

It had been a game. He'd found her secret phone on day one, right after he discovered she was missing, and had called her, tricking her into redirecting her messages to his Inbox. And she'd been none the wiser. Mostly she'd been asking about his team members.

"So why the renewed interest in me?" he wondered aloud. He rejoined his family, half listening to the wedding chatter since he was busy formulating a way to turn the tables on the overly curious Agent Barnes.

"YOU'RE GOING TO WEAR out the carpet," Martin muttered as he peered around J.J. to catch the late fourth-quarter play on the television.

"Yeah," Denise chimed in. "What's with all the pacing?"

Lara looked up from her find-a-word book and added, "It is annoying, Barnes. Can't you just sit down and read a magazine or something?"

"No." J.J. planted her hands on her hips and blew out a breath of frustration. "I'm tired of being cooped up in here. Can't we go into town?"

"No." It was a consensus.

"What about a walk outside?"

"*Again* with the great outdoors stuff?" Lara groaned.

"Snow's too deep for a walk," Denise pointed out. "And Cody took the SUV."

Cody the turncoat! she wanted to shout. Okay, so maybe that was jumping to conclusions, but she was feeling pretty damned jumpy. "I'm going insane here, folks. Let's go out and rig up a sled, build a snowman, decorate the stables, dig a ditch—*anything!* Have mercy, I beg you. I need *exercise.* I have to look at *something* besides these walls."

"Look outside," Lara said with a jerk of her head toward the window. "Snow and trees as far as the eye can see. And frigging *cold.* You're nuts if you want to go out there. Run up and down the stairs until the idea passes why don't you?"

"Can't walk in it, and we don't have any transportation," Denise said sympathetically. "Sorry, Barnes, you're stuck in here for the duration. Be a brave little toaster."

"Actually, we *do* have transportation. There are several snowmobiles in the garage," normally quiet Martin suggested, glancing up from the TV.

"No way," Lara choked. "Post-op girl probably shouldn't be on a bumpy snowmobile and Cody said to stick close."

Snowmobile? Sounded like a possibility. A good one. So good that J.J. was willing to get down on her knees and beg. Turned out it wasn't necessary.

Martin switched off the television. "What would it hurt?" he asked. "We go slow, take in the sights. It might do us all some good to get out for a while." He glanced over at J.J. and asked, "Assuming you're up to it?"

"I'm not up to it," Lara said. "I'll freeze inside an hour."

"So we'll keep it short," Martin offered. "Down to the ravine and back. It's forty minutes tops. Cody said he had them gassed up, so, Denise, you in?"

"Why not," she answered. "Just gotta go upstairs and get my boots."

"Lara?"

"Okay. But I've got to go upstairs and put on three more layers of clothing. And—" she stopped in the archway leading to the stairs "—if Cody finds out, you take full responsibility."

"Not a problem," Martin insisted easily, grinning at J.J. "Cody's a decent guy. Lara just doesn't know him well enough."

While J.J. was putting on her coat and lacing her boots, she seized the opportunity to talk for a few minutes alone with Martin after Denise went to the rest room. "You sound as if you know Cody well."

"Going on fifteen years. I was his mentor when he first joined the Marshal Service."

So how come he outranks you? she wondered. "He's not a very hands-on team leader, is he?"

"Sure he is," Martin countered. J.J. believed the answer was honest and heard the respect and open admiration in his tone. "Cody *is* the job. He's given one hundred percent to it from day one."

"And you haven't?"

Martin looked down to tie his laces. "For the most part. I got married a few years ago. You know how it is. The job changes when you're not single anymore. That's why I'm getting out."

That was news. "You're quitting?"

He laughed. "Retiring, young lady. I've got my twenty years in next month. My wife and I are moving to a little place in Idaho. Maybe start that family we've been talking about all these years. Didn't seem right to do it when I was always traveling."

Buying a house? That could be motive for selling out the other witnesses. "Big place for lots of kids?"

He grunted. "Small place. I'm a government employee and my wife's a secretary. It's nice, though," he insisted, fumbling for his wallet and producing a photograph of a modest home in a modest neighborhood.

The house appeared to be an easily affordable option for a dual-income couple with no kids. Kinda shot her theory all to hell.

"Martin boring you with the house pictures?" Denise asked when she rejoined them.

"Excuse me," Martin snipped good-naturedly. "Unlike Denise, *I* didn't marry an entrepreneur. Her husband figured out a way to make a mint on the Internet."

Denise swatted Martin's head. "It's not a mint, you moron. He traded stocks online. No big deal and certainly none of *her* business."

J.J. didn't blame Denise for being pissed. But she appreciated the information all the same. So, Denise's husband was making lots of money. That could either eliminate her as a suspect or put her at the top of the list. Sometimes a little money made people want a lot of money. It was another angle.

A few moments later, they were on their way, with Lara complaining on the short walk to the garage. It was too cold. She'd never been on a snowmobile. They could get lost. The world could end.

"Give it a rest, Selznick," Martin insisted as he started pulling tarps off the snowmobiles. "Think of this as an opportunity to learn a new skill. You're always complaining about never being given challenges. Well, this is one."

"I meant *professional* challenges," Lara corrected, moving over to where Martin was standing to affix the goggles he'd retrieved from the handle of the machine. "I want this one."

"They're all the same," he argued.

"This one is bigger," she insisted. "If I'm going to do this, I'm going to do it right."

"Since you've never done it," Martin countered, "I'd suggest you take one of the others."

"Let her have it," Denise called. "You know our Lara. She always has to do things the hard way."

Were these people always so contentious? J.J. wondered. Not to mention annoying. They debated everything, from the order of their showers to what to make for dinner. Hardly a cohesive team. It was yet another failing on Cody's part. He should be here. These people definitely needed supervision. Or a collective swift kick.

In deference to her recent medical problems—which Cody had, thankfully, covered by blaming her previous surgery—they departed the garage and took off at a leisurely pace toward the eastern edge of the property. The pastureland butted the foothills, providing a natural barrier, should the Visnopovs be thinking of dropping by.

The hum of the engine lulled J.J. into her private

thoughts. Jumbled as they were. Of the four suspects, she didn't want to acknowledge that Cody was the strongest by a long shot.

The business card she'd discovered was the most incriminating evidence of all. That and the little bit of the phone conversation she'd overheard had put him at the top of her list.

It just didn't feel right to her. She couldn't fathom a single reason why Cody would jump into bed with the Russian mob. He seemed like a decent guy. More than decent, actually. He'd kept her secret. And he'd consoled her. Definite pluses. Why would a guy who was orchestrating her execution do either of those things? It didn't make sense.

Then again, neither did Martin as the leak. He was on the verge of retirement and apparently planning on spending it in a quiet place with a nice wife and some nice kids. Denise had given her little to nothing to arouse her suspicions. And then there was Lara. She was definitely hiding something—but a link to the mob seemed like a huge stretch.

Which brought her back to Cody as they arrived at an uphill slope at the base of the mountains. Cutting the motor, J.J. shoved off her goggles and dismounted, awed by the beauty.

"There was no hiking mentioned," Lara griped as she got off her snowmobile, then planted her feet in the snow, her arms crossed. "The higher the elevation, the more wind. More wind means a drop in temperatures."

"Just a little ways up," J.J. implored. "Just high enough to get a view of the sun starting to set."

"Come on, Lara," Martin urged. "You might like it."

"I'll hang back here, thank you very much." Lara remained anchored in place.

"Suit yourself." Martin shrugged. "I wonder if the camera on my cell phone is decent enough to get a picture of this."

"That would be great," J.J. said with genuine enthusiasm.

Martin took the lead. Which made sense. As the heaviest, he could test the footing. The terrain was a pretty slick mixture of rock, ice and snow as the three of them snaked their way higher.

The only sounds were the occasional flutter of a bird overhead and the echoes of Lara slapping her arms to keep warm. There was an earthy smell that reminded J.J. of childhood camping trips. And had her suddenly longing for a gooey s'more. Somewhere higher up in the rocks, a deer skittered, faltered on a rock, then bounded off for the relative safety of some undergrowth. The aroma of pine grew stronger the higher they went.

"I think this is far enough," Martin said as he turned and rested against a boulder. "Wow. Now that's a once in a lifetime sight."

J.J. turned and had to agree. It was as if someone had taken a broad brush and painted swatches of pinks, purples, yellows and golds across the endless sky interrupted only by the mountains. All of the colors converged on the giant sun just beginning to hide behind the tallest of the peaks.

"Let's see if this thing can do this justice," Martin said, flipping open the phone and pointing it toward the scene. "Too bad it doesn't have a wide-angle lens," he joked, adjusting the phone so J.J. could see the preview in the two-inch screen.

"It's great," she promised, touching his forearm as she offered a reassuring smile. "And it's the only option we have."

"Make it a speedy option," Denise cautioned. "We don't really want to be out here much longer. It's starting to get dark, and Lara's freezing."

"One sec and we'll be on our way," Martin promised. "One…two…"

He never got to say three. Or if he did, it was drowned out by the sound of an explosion.

Chapter Seven

"Remote detonation," Seth confirmed.

For the second time in only seven days, Cody was standing in the hallway of Community Hospital with his gut in a knot. "Send the stuff to the lab in Helena," he told his brother. Then he turned, his gaze seeking out J.J. He walked over to her and didn't even try to hide his annoyance. "You. Follow me."

Stomping down the corridor, he checked doors until he found an empty room. He went inside, pulling J.J. along with him. "What the hell were you thinking?"

She flinched. It was quick and she recovered quickly, but at least he figured he had her full attention. "Well?"

Brushing hair away from her face, J.J. met his gaze. "I'm sorry Lara was hurt. Thank God it was just a minor break and a concussion, not something a lot worse. But it was an innocent trip, Landry. We all agreed to—"

"You got one of my team members blown up! Don't try to minimize it. Rule number one has always been that you don't leave the house without my express permission." Cody let out a frustrated breath and fought off a compelling urge to punch a hole in the closest wall. He was too furious to even look at her.

"I accept full responsibility for the incident. You're right. It was stupid of us to go out. But, dammit, Landry, we all had cabin fever. Besides," she continued hotly, "your express permission doesn't mean a whole lot when you're always off with The Brady Bunch."

"Incident?" He felt his eyes narrow as his blood began to boil. "Don't you dare question my handling of this assignment, Barnes."

The smart move would have been to back away, but Barnes took a different tack. She got right in his face. Her breath washed over his throat. "Why not? So far, I haven't seen much in the way of leadership from you, Landry. No wonder you keep losing your protectees. You're never around to protect anyone."

Forget impulse control. Cody slammed his fist into the wall to the left of her head. The drywall caved from the force.

J.J. grunted her disgust and made a production out of putting her hands on her hips. She looked like an irritated parent about to chastise an errant child. Didn't do much to improve his temper.

"Feel better now?" J.J. said evenly. She hadn't even flinched as his fist came within inches of her head. "Hitting things is never a solution. It won't unbreak Lara's collarbone nor will it cure her concussion. And it certainly won't tell us how the snowmobile ended up rigged with potassium nitrate, charcoal and sulfur."

Furrowing his brow, he felt his anger dissipate. Intrigue replaced it, as he tried to figure out how she knew so much so soon. "Guessing, or do you want to share how you know the components of the—"

"Hardly a psychic revelation moment, Landry. I was there, I smelled the blast. It was gunpowder. Since I neither saw nor heard a flash prior to the explosion, it had to be detonated by a signal or timer."

"Remote job," he confirmed. "Bomb squad found enough in the debris to confirm that much."

She took in a deep breath, held it for a second, then exhaled. "Inside job."

Cody's chest tightened hearing her say what he didn't want to hear. Even if it was the most logical explanation. Problem was, he couldn't tell her that the perimeter of the farmhouse wasn't completely secure or that he'd been absent a lot because he couldn't stomach the notion of hanging her out to dry. He couldn't tell her without disobeying orders. Even ones he fervently disagreed with.

"Looks like. But can't be. I trust my team."

"I'd trust only Lara and Martin if I were you."

He speared her with a look. "Why just the two of them? Why not trust *all* of us?"

J.J. put up a hand. "Hear me out, okay?" She explained how the two had argued over the rigged snowmobile which made it pretty unlikely that either knew it was potentially fatal. "So that leaves Denise." Her lashes fluttered briefly before she added, "And you."

"Me, huh?"

She nodded. "In fact, you're at the top of my list."

"I am, am I? In that case you're pretty stupid to be standing here—alone—with a murderer, and a mad bomber, aren't you? What's to say I won't kill you right here and now, Agent Barnes? If I wanted to hurt you, J.J., I've had lots of opportunities." He stepped closer until she was trapped between the wall and his body. He was cautious to keep a single hair's space between them. Flattening his palms on either side of her head, he dipped his head, bringing them almost nose to nose.

Her nose was perfect, he noted. Small and precisely centered above her full, rosy lips. He smelled soap, but not fear. There wasn't so much as an inkling of hesitation in those clear, stunning eyes. J.J. Barnes wasn't a woman prone to intimidation.

"Ditto," she returned.

He smiled. It had been nearly imperceptible, but he heard the evidence that she wasn't quite as self-assured as she appeared. Nor as immune to him as she wanted him to believe.

"Really?"

Cody relaxed a bit and was feeling pretty cocky. Until he felt a sharp pain in his arm, another in his calf, and then realized he was lying flat on his back. J.J. Barnes had dropped him like a bad habit and he hadn't seen it coming.

His ego hurt almost as much as his back. Correction. More.

Reaching out a hand to him, she did nothing to keep the smug smile from her face. "Any more questions?"

He shook his head as he stood without her assistance. "Pretty much cleared that issue right up for me."

"Fine. So explain to me why I shouldn't think of you as my prime suspect." Moving to the bed, J.J. sat on the edge and hoped he wouldn't figure out that tossing him to the ground had sapped a good portion of her strength.

Cody pulled a chair close to the bed and sat. Rubbing his shoulder, he said, "Because I'm willing to admit to being distracted, but I'd never, *ever,* put you or any member of my team in danger."

"Distracted by what?"

"It's personal."

Personal as in girlfriend? What? "If you want me to move on, then I need more than that. C'mon, Landry. You're one of only two people who know about…about my attack. I trusted you with that information, so I think it's your turn to show some good faith."

He offered a sheepish grin. "If I don't, are you going to toss my butt onto the tile floor again?"

She found his smile contagious. "I might. Whatever it takes to get the job done."

"I've been trying to get a gift for my brother's wedding."

"A wedding gift?" she scoffed. "I got shot at and Lara got blown up because you were shopping for a gift?"

"No. Not shopping, exactly." He turned his dark head, his expression growing distant. In the ensuing silence, it felt as if he no longer realized she was in the room. "My folks took off several years ago. I was too busy, so I hired a private detective to try to track them down. I had hoped to find them in time for this wedding."

Wow. "Took off?" she asked. It didn't fit with what little she knew. The Landrys seemed to be such a close-knit clan.

"I think they were having some problems, then they up and left."

"What kind of problems?"

He shrugged. The action caused the soft fabric of his chambray shirt to pull taut against his broad chest. She knew she shouldn't be distracted; she just couldn't help it. *How sick was that?* Here he was spilling his guts and she was lusting over him. *Focus, Agent Barnes. Focus.*

"Stuff," was his evasive answer. "They were my parents. They didn't exactly seek out my counsel."

"Come on, Cody," she said, leaning forward to rest her hand on his knee. "You and I both know people go missing by choice every day of every year for all sorts of reasons."

"I know." He sighed. "Just not *my* folks."

"You said they were having problems. Maybe they needed some space." *When did I start channeling Dr. Phil?*

"For more than ten years?" he countered, obviously frustrated. "I could buy it if nothing much had happened in all those years. Marriages, births. I can't imagine them missing all that. Hell, Clayton went to prison for murder. He was later exonerated, but it doesn't make sense that my parents wouldn't so much as send a note during the trial or after his conviction."

J.J.'s brain whirled as she considered possibilities. One was particularly obvious. Squeezing his knee gently, she quietly asked, "Could they be dead, Cody? Maybe an accident and—"

"No notification?" he cut in. "I've contacted every jurisdiction in this country. No matches. Not as a couple and not as individuals. It's like they dropped off the face of the earth."

"Maybe they went out of the country."

"That's why I called Wilkofski," he explained.

"Wilkofski is your P.I.?" *That explains the card taped to the wardrobe. Kinda.*

He nodded and she saw a spark in his eye. "Yep, it's a firm with contacts all over the globe. One of his operatives might be on to something, but he probably can't track it down in time for the wedding on Saturday."

She felt her heart tug at the sound of utter disappointment in his voice. "So, you'll keep at it and in the meantime, you'll buy a place setting like every other self-respecting wedding guest."

The smile that reached all the way to his eyes made her stomach clench.

"How about I call in some favors?" she said. "See if the FBI can come up with anything?"

"I've tried that."

"I'm sure you have," she agreed as she patted his muscular thigh. "But I've got a slight advantage over you. I've got some people who owe me favors. It can't hurt, right?"

His hand slipped over hers, sending a shock the full length of her arm. "Thanks, J.J., really."

"No problem," she said through the tightness in her throat. Halfheartedly, she attempted to pull her hand away. "You can let go now."

"Yeah, I can," he replied, though he kept his hand in place.

The soft, husky sound of his voice resonated through

every cell in her body. All of her thoughts should have been focused on the investigation. But they weren't. Not by a long shot.

Ever so gently, Cody urged J.J. from the bed, into the V of his thighs. Words scrolled through his mind like a marquee— Wrong. Stop. Don't. Shouldn't. He ignored them all.

Instead he slid his hands over the sides of her legs until his fingers gripped the smallness of her waist. He scanned her face, looking for even the smallest hint that his attentions might be unwanted. Relief filled him when he saw curiosity smoldering in her incredible eyes.

His pulse increased in correlation with his interest. Slipping his thumbs beneath the hem of her shirt, he felt the warm, silky softness of her skin. That alone was enough to ignite a fiery passion in the pit of his stomach. J.J. dipped her head, her full lips coming dangerously close to his.

Purposefully Cody countered the move, wanting— no *needing*—to make this moment last. He wanted to imprint every second on his brain. The feel of her skin, the erratic rhythm of her breathing, the lilac scent of her hair, the anticipation in her gaze. All of it mattered. He knew the kiss would be the end and he wanted to postpone that for as long as possible.

Slowly he began making small circles with his thumbs against her skin as he squeezed his thighs, trapping her in place. He watched, fascinated, as her lips parted and a faint, telling moan spilled from her mouth. Her hands went to his shoulders, her fingers digging into him as he teased the pad of his thumb a fraction of an inch below her waistband.

J.J.'s grip became more insistent and she again tried to brush her lips against his. Not yet.

Cody countered by placing his mouth against the base of her throat, tasting the warm skin. He heard her breath catch as his tongue darted out to flick the pulse point on her neck. She pressed closer, hindered by his tight control over her ability to move. Feeling the full, soft roundness of her breasts against his chest, he nearly abandoned his plan for a slow, patient approach.

He worked a deliberate path up her throat, teasing and nibbling sexy little sounds from her as he went. When he reached her jawline, he spent extra time there, tasting and kissing her heated skin.

Lifting his hands from her waist, he cupped her face in his palms and angled her head toward him, careful to keep just a whisper of distance between them. Hesitating, he studied the hooded passion in her eyes, the way her pupils constricted with each labored, uneven intake of breath. Kissing one cheek, then the other, he rubbed his thumb along her bottom lip.

Her mouth opened wider as her tongue flicked out and touched the pad of his finger.

Need stabbed through him. How could such a simple action cause such a strong reaction? His body turned into an electrified jumble of cells, all wanting and needing one thing. Her.

His commendable self-restraint was fading quickly. Replaced by raw, primal passion. Blood pumped through his veins, carrying his desire to every inch of his being. His own heart pounded against his ribs as he fought to retain the last vestiges of control.

It would have worked. He was a decent guy, not some animal. At least he wasn't until J.J. pulled one of her role-reversal moves.

Lacing her fingers through his hair, J.J. pulled Cody to her, crushing his mouth with her own. There was nothing tentative or speculative about the kiss. She made sure of that. Cody had set her body on fire and she was determined to do the same for him.

It didn't take much. Adrenaline and desire fed her strength as she pushed past the grip of his thighs until she was finally able to feel the full press of his body. All the while, she greedily tasted and unabashedly enjoyed his mouth.

Incredible. That was the only word to describe the magical feelings churning inside her. Need, curiosity, passion, frustration—all fueled by the feel of him. She wasn't quite sure what she wanted or in what order. Only that she wanted more. Much, much more.

"Hang on," Cody breathed into her mouth.

Reason intruded into her consciousness. "Right," she agreed, "the door. I'll lock the door."

J.J. half-turned when Cody caught her wrist and then held her gaze. His hair was tousled and sexy and, if she did say so herself, the man looked thoroughly kissed. She smiled at him, enjoying the anticipation tingling all through her.

"Don't lock the door."

So Cody had a wild side, eh? "But someone could walk in."

Lifting her hand to his mouth, he placed a kiss on her palm that made her want to swoon on the spot. "I'm not worried about someone walking *in*. I'm telling you that we should be *walking out*."

"Out?" she repeated as if he'd said it in tongues.

Cody rose slowly. He had that look. It was the I'm-about-to-reject-you look.

She yanked her hand free and all but jumped as far away from him as possible. *Boy, did I get that all wrong!*

Closing her eyes tightly, she braced herself for his rejection as she prayed for inner strength. Please do not let my utter humiliation show.

"J.J., we can't do this."

Crossing her arms, she willed her heart rate back to normal. "You're right. It was a stupid lapse of judgment on my part. It was unfair of me to use you to feel better about myself."

He cocked his head and his lips drew into a thin line. "Are you telling me that was some sort of exercise in emotional healing?"

She covered with a nervous laugh. "Of course. I was the victim of an assault, so on some level, I guess I needed to know I was still capable of summoning up a normal physical reaction to a man."

Shaking his head, he smirked at her. "The only problem with that lame comment is that *I* know you don't remember the assault."

"That doesn't mean I don't have…issues."

"The only issues you have, Barnes, are poor timing and a doctor's note. I'm a patient guy, so don't think for a minute that this—" he wagged his forefinger between them "—is finished."

"In your dreams."

"Really?" he taunted, one dark brow arched. "Five minutes and I could have you begging me."

"To stop? *That* you could manage in about ten seconds."

He chuckled. "Every chance I get, I'll be reminding you that it was your idea to toss the gauntlet, Barnes."

"Who needs a gauntlet, Landry? Right now I'd be willing to toss pretty much anything at you."

"That's because you can't stand the fact that I'm right."

"Right annoying."

"Try being honest for a change. You want me, Barnes."

"I do *not* want you. And I *am* honest."

"Really? Then why did you melt in my arms?"

"Did not." *Lord, I sound like I'm in kindergarten!*

"We will argue our mutual attraction another time in another place. As for your honesty, at what point were you going to tell me your real reason for being here?"

Her throat went dry. "My reason is to stay alive until the Visnopov trial."

"And?" he prodded.

Her eyes narrowed. "And nothing."

He shrugged, turned his back to her and started for the door. "Too bad, Barnes. If you'd have opened up to me, I might have told you about the date on the back of the card you found when you searched my room this morning."

Chapter Eight

Cody, J.J. and his now two-person team piled into the SUV later that night and headed north, to the only safe house he could find on short notice.

It was a small homestead on the south edge of the Lucky 7. It had been built in the late 1960s for a long-time employee of the Landry family. It was the kind of thing his folks had done, Cody thought with a renewed pang of melancholy—reward loyalty.

Shane was waiting for them, his brow beaded with sweat, leaning against the handle of the snow shovel he'd used to clear the walkway.

"How's the girl—Lara?"

"She'll be fine, just out of commission for a few days," Cody replied as he slung his bag over his shoulder and led the group to the modest building. "Thanks for your help on this."

"Don't thank him. He actually did very little," Taylor announced as she came out the front door, tugging a large sweater over her shoulders. "I've stocked the fridge and there's some stew heating on the stove. Rolls are in the oven."

"Three hours of manual labor and I got nothing. Squat. Nada," Shane griped. "Not even water."

"Show some initiative, Shane. If you were thirsty, you could have sucked on snow," she remarked as she jabbed at his ribs before bounding down the steps.

"She's always hitting me."

"Remind you of old times?"

"Yeah. Tortured by brothers as a child and now I'm stuck with Taylor the Terrible."

Cody grinned and patted his brother's shoulder. "Be brave."

Digging into the front pocket of his jeans, Shane just grunted as he withdrew his keys, then walked to the truck parked off to the side. It was equipped with a plow, a necessity for Montana winters. Before getting into the cab, he called out, "You be safe."

Let's hope. Cody ushered everyone inside. Unlike the Simms farm house, this was a small, two-room structure. He guessed the lingering scent of cleaning solution was courtesy of Taylor, as was the mouthwatering smell of the stew simmering on the stove.

The living room—kitchen combo featured a dinette set, chair, coffee table, tattered plaid sofa and a television that looked like it belonged in the Smithsonian. Predictably, Martin honed in on that fact.

The adjoining bedroom had either twin beds or two cots, depending on a person's level of optimism. The bathroom was little larger than a closet—shower, toilet and a small sink with the enamel chipped along the edge.

"Sorry," he said as he moved behind J.J, who seemed to be taking everything in.

She shrugged. "I've been in worse. It has running water and it's warm. All a girl needs for a decent night's sleep."

"All a prairie girl needs," Denise griped. "Jeez, Landry, couldn't we drive to a motel or something?"

"This is the place," he announced in his best command voice. "Make the best of it."

They ate in relative silence, then decided on the shifts for what was left of the night. Martin stretched out on the sofa. J.J. and Denise took the bedroom. Cody was too wired to sleep. Taking a mug of coffee, he grabbed his coat and went out onto the porch.

The sky twinkled with stars for as far as the eye could see. It reminded him of his childhood when he and his brothers would play a version of connect-the-dots with the stars. He sighed and dumped the cold remains of the coffee onto the snow below the railing. That memory seemed like a lifetime ago.

Hearing a creak behind him, he spun, and had his gun out and pointed at J.J.'s surprised expression. "You shouldn't sneak up on a person."

"Sorry," she said, arms raised as far as the blanket wrapped around her shoulders would allow. "I can't sleep."

"You should. You need your rest."

Well, that ship pretty much sailed when I started to replay our kiss over and over. "I've been thinking," she began as she moved beside him, careful to make sure her body didn't touch his.

"Is that a positive or negative thing?"

She smiled and felt some of the tension in her muscles relax. "A productive thing." Leaning against the weatherworn rail, she gazed up at the millions of stars and quietly marveled at their beauty. Crisp air filled her lungs, condensing into a faint white stream with each exhale. "Something isn't right around here."

"Took an explosion for you to get that, did it?"

She liked the sound of his teasing voice. It was a deep, resonant sound that had the ability to melt her defenses. "What you said at the hospital was true."

He inched closer. "That I could make you beg?"

Soft laughter spilled from her lips. "Focus, Landry. I'm trying to tell you that I agree we shouldn't be enemies." She felt his eyes on her even before she turned to look up at him.

By moonlight, he was even more devastatingly handsome. By moonlight *with* a relaxed grin, he was downright heart-stopping. It was probably below freezing, but having Cody smile down at her warmed her from the inside out.

"So what should we be?" he asked, reaching out and brushing a few strands of hair from her face.

J.J. reveled in the feel of his large fingers against her skin and struggled to keep from leaning into his touch. The memory of his kiss was fresh in her mind. Well, not just her mind. He was imprinted on her cells. There wasn't a part of her that didn't long to be in his arms. To pick up where they'd left off. *Focus, Barnes!*

"Partners," she explained, watching as her proposal caused undeniable hesitation. "Hear me out."

"There are no partners between a marshal and a protectee, J.J. It doesn't work that way."

"Silent partners, then," she corrected. "Listen, Cody,

please?" When he didn't say anything, she continued. "You aren't going to like this."

"I already don't like it," he retorted wryly.

"I'm more than your protectee."

"That was clear when we kissed."

Okay, so he was going to make this as difficult as possible. Great. She tilted her head back and glared up at him. "Forget the kiss for now. This isn't easy for me and you're making it even harder."

He had the good sense to look apologetic. "Go ahead. According to you, you're more than my protectee, and…"

Why did he have to be cute and annoying all at the same time? "The Visnopov thing taught me an important lesson."

"Which was?"

"I didn't alert any backup that night."

"Not too smart."

"So, the best way to flush out the leak is to work together on—"

His whole demeanor changed. "When I agreed that the explosion at the Simms place might be an inside job, I meant inside on *your* end, not mine."

"*My* end? That doesn't make sense, Landry. The FBI needs me to make the Visnopov case."

"So does the Marshal Service."

Planting her feet slightly apart, she felt irritation rushing though her veins. "Really?" she began, ticking things off on her fingers. "Then how is it your team has lost three witnesses? Allowed me to be shot at *and* had one of your own nearly blown to bits?" Sensing that her logic had tempered his simmering anger, she continued.

"I'm putting myself out here, Landry. I should be reporting that you're the most likely leak, but instead I'm hoping we can work this through together. Find out who the turncoat is and make sure they suffer dearly for switching sides."

"There's a flaw in your theory, Barnes."

"Really?"

"It assumes that I agree with your assessment that one of my team members is the leak."

"Maybe not," she relented. It was a debate tactic since she *did* believe it was one of them. "What if it's someone higher up? Maybe one of the suits in D.C. is selling you out?"

"Besides me there are only three people who know the logistics on any given assignment," he explained. "And I'd trust all of them with my life."

"Good for you," she shot back, "but it's *my* life we're talking about. And I'm not quite as willing to blindly trust anyone who has the ability to get me killed."

"What is it you want from me?" he asked.

"An open mind, Landry. Let me do a little digging and then we'll talk again. I'll need access to Marshal Service files. *Unfettered* access."

"You won't find anything."

Smiling sweetly, she said, "Then think how much fun you'll have gloating at my folly."

"I'M ON IT," Denise said, not bothering to hide the fact that she was thrilled with her assignment. "What's the radius?"

Cody leaned back in the chair, lacing his fingers behind his head. "Twenty miles or less. Go into town and

stop by Seth's office. He's got a list of possible locations we can use for our next safe house."

J.J. noticed the way his biceps strained against his
shirt even though she was supposed to be focusing on
the morning briefing.

"Martin, a rental car is coming in about an hour. Head
up to the crime lab in Helena and get them moving on
the forensics from the shooting and the explosion."

"Doesn't that leave us stuck here with no transportation?" J.J. asked, treading that fine line between challenging him and letting him know she didn't want to be
stranded at the deserted cabin.

"You're not part of this discussion, Barnes."

Cody's dismissive tone grated. J.J. stood and
marched into the bedroom, slamming the door for effect. Apparently their late night tête-à-tête hadn't done
much good. So much for extending olive branches to the
bullheaded jerk.

After locking the door, she pulled out her cell phone
and found she had a message waiting.

SELZNICK, LARA. BACKGROUND, CLEAR. HOW-
ARD, DENISE. BACKGROUND, CLEAR. LANDRY,
CODY. BACKGROUND, CLEAR. NEWELL, MARTIN.
BACKGROUND, CLEAR.

"Thanks for that useless info dump," she grumbled
as she formulated her reply.

Request forward of actual information. Barnes out.

Something wasn't right. Her boss had been down-right chatty for days, then this. It didn't make any sense. "Why no information on the P.I. firm?" she whispered, checking the text function to see if perhaps she'd missed a transmission. Nothing. This text messaging wasn't immediate enough. First chance she got, J.J. was going to call Associate Director Andrews.

A series of knocks on the door sent her scurrying to tuck the cell phone into her sock.

"J.J.?"

Taking a deep, calming breath before opening the door, she felt ready to confront Cody. "Yes?" she asked in a clipped tone, refusing to open the door more than a crack.

"We've got to get going."

"Going where? You dispatched our only means of transportation," she reminded him, making a point of exaggerating her sarcasm.

He let out an annoyed breath as he shoved open the door and tossed her coat at her. "Give me some credit, Barnes. Let's go."

Waiting out front was a black Hummer with the en-gine running. "Where'd you get this?"

"One of the perks of having more brothers than a fra-ternity house," he quipped as he slipped behind the wheel.

"Where are we going?"

"Off road," he answered as he shifted the gigantic ve-hicle into four-wheel drive.

Gripping the dashboard, J.J. lurched from side to side as Cody followed some secret road heading north. "Are the highways closed?"

"Nope." He continued to spin the steering wheel as

he negotiated the seemingly impassable terrain. "The back way is quicker."

"The back way to what, *exactly?*"

"The ranch."

"As in your family ranch? That isn't a good idea, Cody. What if something happens and—"

"The place is empty. Molly and Chandler asked everyone in the family to be at the church today for a run-through. It wasn't available tomorrow, so it was moved up."

She smiled. "It's called a rehearsal. Why aren't you there?"

He shrugged. "Much to my future sister-in-law's chagrin, I explained that I am perfectly capable of ushering women to their seats even without several hours of practice."

"But this is a family thing. You don't want to make them mad, do you?"

"They'll get over it," he insisted. "The house has everything we need to access the information you seem to think will hang one of my team members. I figure it will be easier on me to let you get this theory out of your system."

"That was pretty patronizing," she said. She would have said more, but she was distracted by the sight of the house coming into view.

A sprawling clapboard home rivaled the beauty and majesty of the mountains in the distance. Cody veered to the right, driving along a fence line that seemed to go on endlessly. Twisting in her seat, she kept the house in sight. Awestruck, she couldn't imagine actually living in a place like this.

The Hummer cleared the arched iron sign with the Lucky 7 logo, putting them on the slippery gravel driveway that formed a horseshoe at the base of a half-story staircase leading to a broad, wraparound porch.

Beyond the house were corrals, barns and other buildings she couldn't identify by name, thanks to her limited knowledge of ranch life.

"Wow."

Cody looked over and seemed amused by her reaction. "Welcome to the Lucky 7."

Stepping out of the car, she tilted her head back and took in the grandeur of the place. "It looks more like a bed-and-breakfast than a home."

"It *is* more of a bed-and-breakfast," he joked, taking her hand and leading her up the steps. "I'll give you a quick tour before we get to work."

She squeezed his hand. "I'm impressed. Are the Landrys the Trumps of the west?"

"Hardly."

Shoving one of the double doors open, Cody dropped her hand, stepped aside and allowed her to enter the house first.

"Wow."

"This," he began, "is the foyer. Perfectly designed for a game of sock hockey."

J.J. smiled, imagining Cody and his brothers sliding up and down the hardwood floors. "I'm sure your parents must have loved that."

"They didn't mind."

She glanced questioningly at him.

He shrugged, adding, "They believed a house should

be lived in. So long as we stayed out of the sacred rooms, we pretty much had the run of the place."

"Sacred rooms?"

"Pop's office, mom's parlor and the master bedroom."

"Got it," J.J. said, distracted by the antique light fixture overhead. "Tiffany?"

"Handel," he corrected. "Tiffany Lite. Or so I'm told. First floor or second floor?"

Spying the carved mahogany staircase, she pointed in its direction. "Wow," she repeated as they climbed the steps toward the picture window with the unobstructed view of the Rockies.

"Your college education isn't showing right now, Barnes."

"My modest beginnings are," she readily admitted. "I grew up in a tiny apartment in Atlanta. The closest I ever came to a house like this was a class field trip. Even then, we were kept behind ropes and only allowed to look." Spotting the elegant master bedroom after they'd reached the second floor, she again whispered, "Wow. It's immaculate. Taylor's doing, I'm guessing?"

"Partly," he answered, his eyes suddenly clouded with emotion. "A lot of us still think of it as our folks' room."

He hurried her down the hallway. "This mess belongs to Shane."

J.J. fought back a laugh. "Everything else is so neat. Why does this room look like it hasn't been cleaned?"

"Standoff. From what I've been able to pick up here and there, Taylor refuses to do anything for Shane until he apologizes."

"For what?"

"Who knows?"

He moved on, showing her no fewer than six bedrooms and four bathrooms. Each room had an individual personality. Some feminine, some decidedly masculine. One was an adorable nursery, decorated with bunnies and birds in soft pastels. J.J. stopped in the doorway of the nursery, trying to make sense of the sudden rush of strong emotion.

"Sam and Callie are moving out as soon as their place is—"

J.J. barely heard him. She just knew that her chest was tight and a huge lump threatened to choke off her air. Pivoting on her heel, she pushed past him and raced down the stairs.

"J.J.?"

Cody could have kicked himself, but he was in too much of a rush to catch up with her. She must think he was an insensitive jerk.

Reaching her on the next to last step, he grasped her shoulders and turned her into him. She was stiff in his arms as her forehead rested against his shoulder.

"I don't know what's wrong with me," she said without lifting her head.

Cody stroked her hair. He was completely unsure of the right thing to say or do. Helpless wasn't a feeling he knew well.

"You probably need more time." He shifted her so that her cheek was against his chest. "I'm sorry. I wasn't thinking."

"No, *I'm* sorry," she said as she flattened her palm against his chest. "The kicker is, I've always dismissed the whole motherhood thing. It was something I figured I'd deal with off in the future."

He felt anger surge through him and he struggled to keep the emotion out of his tone. "I'm sorry about what happened, J.J."

"I'm not," she said softly. Moving out of his embrace, she looked up at him. "What kind of person does that make me?" she asked as he watched conflict play across her face. "What kind of woman is relieved because she isn't sure she could have loved her own child?"

Gently he placed his hands against her cheeks. "Any woman faced with having a child as a result of a rape. Don't let yourself think anything different. Okay?"

She took a deep breath and attempted a halfhearted smile. "I guess you're right."

"I'm always right," he joked, hoping to lighten her spirits. "If and when you decide to have a child, it will be *your* decision and you'll celebrate it."

One pale brow arched high on her forehead. "You're some kind of expert on children? Last time I looked, you didn't have any."

"I'm pacing myself," he joked, glad to see the haunted look gone from her pretty eyes. "I'll make some coffee and then we can get to work."

"I'll make the coffee," she insisted, as she followed him into the kitchen.

"Are you mocking my coffee?"

"Pretty much," she said as she accepted a canister and a filter from him. "You and your team make tar. You must have stomachs lined with lead."

"That's pretty harsh, Barnes," he said, secretly agreeing with her.

Cody took a seat and found himself enjoying the sight of J.J. working in the kitchen. Or more accurately, he was enjoying the unobstructed view of her perfectly shaped derriere. Sculpted by formfitting jeans, her body was a true thing of beauty. Tiny waist, slender hips, legs that seemed to go on forever. He couldn't find a single flaw as he watched her move around.

Not that he was really looking for one. Not by a long shot. The more time he spent with J.J., the more he liked and respected her. Maybe his initial assessment of her had been a little harsh. Maybe.

MAKING COFFEE gave J.J. some time to regroup. She'd gone into this mission with a singular goal—find the leak.

She'd also gone into this mission thinking Cody was nothing more than a sexist jerk. Well, she hadn't found the leak and Cody Landry, it turned out, could be a pretty decent guy. Hardly a report she could send to the associate director of the FBI. How did this get so muddled?

Illogical as it sounded, she'd dismissed Cody as a prime suspect on nothing more substantive than her gut reaction. Her boss hadn't exactly been supplying her with a wealth of information. So, after a week in Jasper, she was no closer to finding out who was responsible for the deaths of the three witnesses.

She was climbing out on the tip of a very tenuous branch. Trusting Cody—even just a little—could be a fatal mistake. However, with little to no information coming from her superiors, she didn't really have a choice.

Keeping her back to him, she tried to sound casual when she said, "I've always tried to do my job by the book."

"I got that from day one. And from everything I know, you adhere to that philosophy."

Turning, she met his clear, attentive gaze. "Then you'll appreciate how hard this is for me."

Stretching out his legs, he crossed them at the ankles, then said, "Shoot."

"When I suggested we become partners, I didn't tell you everything."

She saw something flash in his dark eyes. "Really?"

"But before I say anything else, I need a good faith thing from you."

"Such as?"

"The card in your room. Why did you write the date of my attack on the back?"

"I didn't."

She felt her stomach drop. She'd hoped for honesty, needed it if she was going to be completely truthful with him. Well, so much for that.

"Okay." She turned back to the coffeepot and listened to it sputter.

"It wasn't the date of your attack."

She rolled her eyes and willed her temper into check. "I may not remember much about the incident, Landry, but I do recall the date."

"Which just happens to be the same date my parents left. I was scribbling when I talked to the guy on the phone."

"Can you prove that?"

"Yes, if I have to. Do I?"

She thought for a long moment. "Yes."

Cody left the kitchen, then returned a few minutes later with a yellowed newspaper clipping that he shoved under her nose. It confirmed that the senior Landrys hadn't been seen since the night of October 10. Same date. Different year.

Deliberately she turned and met his hostile glare. "Sorry, but I needed that."

"I didn't."

Okay, I deserved that. "Now I'll tell you the real reason I'm here. I wasn't just sent here for you to protect me. The FBI is convinced that you or one of your team members is in the Visnopovs' pocket."

He moved to within inches of her. "What about you? Do you think one of us is on the take?"

Swallowing the rush of fear, she held his piercing gaze and said, "Yes, I agree with that assessment."

Chapter Nine

Cody looked...*wounded* and that had her feeling pretty much like a jerk.

"You agree." His dark chocolate gaze narrowed as Cody flatly repeated, "You...*agree?*"

The tension that her accusation had caused hung in the air between them. Taut and uncomfortable. Since his question was clearly rhetorical, J.J. turned to focus on the final sputterings from the coffeepot instead of the heat of his gaze fixed on her back. She had no idea why she felt like a Judas. Like Cody, she was a public servant. If her boss said jump, she jumped. And darn it, it wasn't as though there wasn't clear evidence that one of his team members was in bed with the bad guys. She was just doing her job. He should be grateful she'd given him a heads-up.

The click of the wall clock marking time echoed in her ears. She sucked in deep breaths, trying to find her center.

After pouring coffee into matching mugs, she went to the table and placed his in front of him, then sat down. His eyes tracked her every movement. It was irritating.

"Stop glaring at me and say something."

"Like what?" he asked, his voice tight.

J.J. raked her fingers through her hair. "Like, 'Gee, Barnes, you may have a point.'"

He brought the mug to his mouth, his expression strained. Allowing the cup to hover just shy of his lips, he said, "Gee, Barnes, you may have a point."

"Your sincerity is lacking."

He swallowed, then sighed deeply. "You're asking me to believe that people I've worked with for years are responsible for at least three deaths."

She leaned forward, touching her fingertips to the back of his hand. His skin was warm. His look was not. "I'm only asking you to *consider* the possibility."

"That's a lot to ask."

There was something in his tone. Not sadness, exactly, but definitely an indication that what she'd said struck a chord. *Good.* "Cody, this is my assignment. It was a breach for me to bring you into the loop. A breach that could get me fired. I'm supposed to be undercover. Sharing my true purpose for being here breaks about a zillion bureau regulations, but I did it. This is *huge* for me."

"I get that." He was still annoyed.

With her? With the assignment? Frustrated, she rose, took the mug to the sink, dumped the coffee and started for the door.

"Wait!" Cody called as he caught up to J.J. Her muscles stiffened beneath his touch. He tried to think of something to say. The truth was out of the question. Stepping around her and planting his palms on her shoulders, he met and held her gaze.

An entire vocabulary of unspoken, angry words glistened in her beautiful eyes. The woman would probably like nothing more than to toss him on his back again. Conflicting emotions churned in his gut. "Okay, okay," he relented. "I brought you here so you could access the Marshal Service database and get this out of your system. I can—"

"Don't patronize me, Landry." She slapped his hands off of her.

"I'm not," he insisted. "Bad choice of words. Can I try again?" He smiled down at her. *Lord,* Cody thought, relieved when he saw a small decrease in her hostility level, *weren't they a fine pair?* Both feeling the sting of their convictions, both defensive when what they really wanted to do was—

Keep your mind on the job, Landry, Cody cautioned himself. Not paying attention in his line of work could get people killed. The Visnopov case had a high enough body count as it was. "Let's go into Sam's office so we can explore your theory. Better?"

"Marginally."

He heard her expel a loud breath and felt the rush of it against his throat. "Cut me some slack, please? I'm trying here."

Slowly resentment seemed to fade from her expression. "Yeah, you're *trying* all right." She didn't exactly exude gratitude, but she no longer looked as if she'd like to whip out her gun and shoot him in the…ba—foot. A grin curved the corners of her pretty mouth.

That simple action and the fact that she'd confided

in him when it could cost her her job—her life—had his brain detouring back into the danger zone.

Dammit!

Hostility he could deal with just fine. But when she looked at him with total, unadulterated faith, every instinct begged for another taste of her. For another chance to feel that incredible mouth against his. *How did she do that? How did she manage to get him from anger, to guilt, to wanting her more than his next breath—all in the blink of an eye? How?*

Because she had the softest skin he'd ever felt. He confirmed his thought by drawing his finger slowly along her jawline. He watched, fixated, as her pupils constricted and her lips parted ever so slightly. She swallowed as the pad of his fingertip glided down her neck, finally resting atop her pulse point, feeling the erratic rhythm.

She made a little sound, something deep and sexy, as her palms flattened against his chest.

J.J. felt the tight, corded muscle and heat of Cody's body beneath her hands. The urgency she felt speeding through her made her head swim, and her thoughts jumble.

Step back, she told herself firmly. *Just step back.* All she had to do was move. One foot, then the other and she'd be out of his force field. Simple. Easy.

Sure, if reason wasn't such a distant second to desire. "I—I think we should go into the office."

The reluctant smile he offered was thrilling. His hands cupped her face and he placed the gentlest of kisses against her forehead. His lips lingered against her skin as he whispered, "You're making me nuts, Barnes. You know that, don't you?"

"Yeah, I do." She felt powerful and giddy all at once. It was a pretty heady combination.

"So what are we gonna do about it?"

"Run up to the first bedroom and—ouch!" He'd spun her around and swatted her fanny. "It was just a suggestion," she offered innocently as he pushed her along the hallway.

"It's cruel the way you're toying with me, Barnes."

"No toying about it," she said, brave because he was behind her and couldn't see her face. There was no way she could speak so openly if they were eye to eye. "I like you, Landry, and…I want you."

He pulled her up short, just shy of a paneled office. His laugh was tinged with what she guessed was a fair amount of frustration. "You really shouldn't admit something like that to a guy who's already hanging by a thread."

Not trusting herself, she rested against the cool wall, trapping her hands behind her body just in case she was overcome by the strong urge to touch him. Again. Peeking up at him through her lashes, she read the frustration carved into his handsome, angled features. "The liking part, or the wanting part?"

"Either. Both."

She shrugged. "Why?"

Rolling his eyes, he balled his hands into fists and shoved them into the front pockets of his jeans. "Because it makes my life really difficult."

She couldn't stop herself from grinning like a giddy

teenager. "Too bad." She poked him in the stomach. "Toughen up, Landry."

"We'll see how tough you are once you no longer have the shield of a doctor's note to hide behind."

She spun away from him and ducked into the office. "I'm not hiding from anything."

"You should be," he insisted. "Any...*involvement* could cost both of us our jobs."

"Could be worth the risk." Despite her resolve to tamp down her urges, she felt possessed by the dangerous need to flex her female power as she watched him round the desk and boot the computer.

"Might very well be," he admitted easily, using two fingers to tap on the keyboard.

Might? Might?

"But we're adults, Barnes. We should both understand and appreciate boundaries."

Boundaries, eh? I'll show you boundaries. J.J., pretending complete interest in the computer screen, leaned *close.* "You have complete access to personnel files?"

He squirmed in the seat as her every word was delivered as a warm breath against his ear. "No. Just my team members." She smiled at the slight crack in his voice. "Who do you want to start with?"

"Hmm..." She practically moaned as she took her sweet time deciding which of the three marshals to pick first. She leaned closer to the computer screen, the action causing her breasts to brush, ever so lightly, against Cody's shoulder. She kept it up until she heard his breathing become slightly more rapid. "Lara. Let's review Lara's file."

Cody tapped a key and then shifted back, allowing her easier access to the monitor.

Keeping her eyes fixed on the screen, J.J. placed her palm on his thigh and peered more closely at the information. "Nothing out of the ordinary," she remarked, glancing at him so that she'd have an excuse for moving her fingers slightly higher on his leg. "Just hard facts."

"Very hard facts."

"I'd like to explore this," she said, pointing toward a page referencing Lara's personal history.

"Explore anything you'd like."

She grinned, liking the fact that his voice was turning into a croak. *Getting to you, eh, Landry?* Applying just a little more pressure against his leg, she leaned over to position the mouse and clicked the link. The computer screen changed and a few paragraphs popped up. "There's not a lot here, is there?"

Suddenly she felt the warmth of his fingers splayed across her rear end. She almost let out a yelp but managed to swallow it in time.

"There's a lot here, J.J.," he countered, slowly exploring the curves of her body. "You're just not processing it because you're too busy trying to seduce me."

Her smugness drained as she turned and found him smirking at her, his dark eyes smoldering as he watched her stumble awkwardly into the desk.

"I wasn't *trying.* I was *succeeding.*"

He shot her a wry smile. "I hate to burst your bubble, but that isn't much of an accomplishment."

She narrowed her eyes. "Are you really going to try

that lame excuse about how *any* man can be seduced by *any* woman at *any* time simply because they're men?"

"No. I'm telling you that it would be easy for you to seduce me because I already want you."

Her eyes widened. "Then how come you were so blasé when I told you I wanted you?"

"Because I'm trying to do the right thing here, Barnes." He reached for her, capturing her hips in his strong grasp. "You're not exactly helping, either. One of us has to be strong, and apparently that person is me."

"I take back what I said before." She crossed her arms in a huff. "I *really* don't like you at all."

He laughed at her. Tossed back his head and belly-laughed at her. And for the first time in more years than she cared to remember, she felt her cheeks burn with a blush.

Indignation and a pretty fair amount of embarrassment replaced every other thought in her head and stiffened her spine. "Can we get back to work now?"

He dropped his hands but his arrogant expression didn't slip an inch. "Absolutely."

J.J. was the picture of professionalism as they spent the better part of two hours on the computer. She read and reread every bit of information on Martin, Cody, Denise and Lara. Nothing jumped out at her. That annoyed her almost as much as Cody's close proximity.

"Anything else before we go back to the cabin?"

She shook her head. "I didn't learn anything new. Unless you count the names of Martin's wife and Denise's husband."

"I could have told you that," he offered as he led her

back through the house. "I was the best man at Martin's wedding. Sally is a lovely lady. Very traditional. Very good for Martin."

"Meaning?" she asked as she slipped on her coat and watched as Cody did the same.

"He needs roots."

She remembered the dossier. "Lost his family in a car accident when he was seventeen. So why'd he wait so long to marry?"

"*Because* he lost his family," Cody explained as he did a visual scan of the area in front of the house. "Clear. Let's go." He escorted her back to the Hummer. "I think he was afraid of what might happen to a wife and kids if he was killed in the line," Cody said, slamming her door.

J.J. saw the logic in that. "What changed his mind?" she asked moments later as he buckled up and started the engine.

"Sally is traditional, but she's also independent. I think Martin knew that if anything happened to him, Sally could go it alone."

"He's retiring."

"Yeah. It's time. He's earned it. And he wants it. But he'll leave some big shoes to fill. He's a good man."

"Denise's husband, Greg—know him?"

She had to wait until Cody negotiated a difficult patch of terrain for an answer. "Not well. Denise is pretty closemouthed about her personal life. I know he's really smart. He can bore you into a stupor explaining stock options."

J.J. smiled. "That would do it for me. Investing isn't one of my strong suits." She quietly admired Cody's profile as he drove the several miles back to the cabin. And she couldn't help but think that this was possibly the last opportunity they'd have to be alone for a while. "I'd have thought someone like you would know all about making money work for you."

"That would be Sam," he insisted. "My oldest brother is a world-class bean counter."

J.J. had seen a photograph of Sam back at the Lucky 7. "He doesn't look like a bean counter."

"Trust me," Cody said with genuine affection in his tone. "I think he wore his first pocket protector to kindergarten. He's a geek through and through."

"So how'd a geek get a stunning wife and two beautiful children?"

"Four," he corrected, telling her about the twins.

"Twins would be scary." She looked up to find him glancing in her direction. "Don't do that, Landry. I'm not going to freak out at the mere mention of babies."

"You did a nice impersonation when you saw the nursery."

She shrugged. "Minor setback. So." She paused when the cabin came into sight, glad that the bumpy ride was about to end. "Tell me about the wedding."

He groaned. "It's in two days—not enough time to recap the festivities."

"Give me the Cliff's Notes."

"Service at the church in town. Reception at the Mountainview Inn."

"See?" She slipped down from the truck and followed Cody up the snowy steps to the cabin. "That wasn't so hard, was it? How many guests?"

"Six hundred."

"People?"

Cody grinned. "Most of them."

He opened the front door and motioned her inside where it was only marginally warmer than outside. His smile dissolved into a frown at the silence that greeted them. "Hang on a sec," he told J.J., reaching for his weapon. "Denise?"

He called out for the other agent again. "Stay here." He moved through the house, weapon raised. But there wasn't anyone inside. He reholstered the gun and walked back into the living room. Denise should have been back by now. Hell, Martin should be back, as well.

"Nobody's here."

J.J. slowly removed her coat. Keeping eye contact with Cody, she let the garment drop to the floor. "Well, darn." Her lips curved into a sexy smile. "Guess we're alone. What *will* we do?"

Chapter Ten

The smart move would have been to resist.

Cody went with his gut.

Drawing J.J. against him, he dropped his head, finding her mouth as his palms laced through her hair and gripped her head.

As his tongue slipped into her mouth, she stepped closer still, flattening herself against him. His body was a tight coil of need as he enjoyed the taste and feel of her. He'd wanted this for what seemed like forever, and the reality exceeded his expectations.

She smelled of fresh air and the subtle fragrance of lavender that clung to her hair. She tasted of the coffee she'd drunk in his family's kitchen, and of desire strong enough to melt the hardest resolve. He couldn't get close enough. He loved the sensations she inspired. On the other hand, he hated the layers of clothing preventing him from experiencing her completely, but was grateful for them at the same time. They reminded him that kissing her was his only option. For now.

J.J. surprised him when she took his hand and flattened it against the swell of her breast. He wasn't sure if he moaned or she did. Probably both. He flicked his thumb across the pebble-hardness of one nipple. Her response was a deliberate brush of her hips against his. His body strained against his jeans. His head was swimming. It was erotic to know that she wanted him as much as he wanted her. As frustrating as it was, knowing they couldn't satisfy their desire for each other only seemed to enhance the experience.

His breath caught when her hand slipped beneath his waistband. Anticipation gripped him as her fingertips reached within a hair of his erection. He felt her smile against his mouth as her fingers slipped lower. *Too much,* his mind screamed. His system was already on overload, despite the fact that they were standing, fully clothed, and they both knew nothing could come of this. Not today.

All rational thought fled as J.J.'s fingers closed around him. This time, he knew the groan was his own. Just as he was sure he was on the verge of something that hadn't happened since high school. He needed to get a grip. Hard to do with her rubbing him while her tongue slowly, teasingly explored his mouth. When her fingers tightened as she sucked on his bottom lip, Cody knew he was a goner. He tried to struggle against his body's reaction, but every nerve and tendon torqued with sweet, intense sensation. He had to—

Had to—

Not wanting her to feel the spasms coursing though him, Cody grit his teeth and gently pushed her away, resting his forehead against hers as he tried to regain his control.

It took him longer than he'd thought it would, but

when his breathing eventually returned to normal, he peered down at her. Lifting his fingertip to her jaw, he asked, "Do I thank you or apologize?"

Getting up on tiptoe, she kissed his cheek and answered, "Neither. You just owe me one."

Wrapping her in his arms, he laughed softly and kissed her head. "Anytime."

"I'll hold you to that." She swatted his rear end. "Now, where were we before?"

J.J. shouldn't have had to remind him. "Denise." He reluctantly let her go, removed his cell from his pocket and dialed. The phone rang half a dozen times before the agent answered. "You shouldn't have left this place unguarded," Cody reminded Denise, trying to keep his annoyance in check as he watched J.J. slip into the bedroom and soundlessly close the door.

He missed her. Gone less than two seconds and he actually missed her. How pathetic was that?

"You're there," Denise replied. "I'm sure Little Miss Feeb is fine in your capable hands."

The sarcasm in her tone didn't improve his mood. "Where are you and what's your ETA?"

"I'm on some back road north of town. Looks like snow rolling in from the west."

"Snow happens," he said, pacing in the small kitchen area. "Any possibilities?"

"With modern plumbing?" Denise answered smartly. "I've seen one ranch house that hasn't been used since, well, *forever.* It's big, but has no central heat and enough cobwebs to make Bela Lugosi proud."

The old Watson place. A favorite hangout for the

Landry boys and their friends to explore as kids. Going inside the abandoned house at midnight was a rite of passage for many Jasper teens. He remembered the experience fondly. It was the first time he knew he could conquer his own fear.

"Cody?"

Blowing out a breath, he asked, "What else?"

"A two-story home at the end of a cul-de-sac in a community near the hospital. It's a pretty populated area, but the houses are—"

"Out of the question. What else?"

She let out an exasperated breath that blasted over the phone line. "Even with Lara down, we *can* secure a location, Cody. Since when do we have to limit our choices to out-of-the-way hovels?"

"Since we lost our last three assignments." Just the hint of losing J.J. made his chest clench. "What else?"

"The Mountainview Inn is nice. It has—"

"Howard, what part of this assignment didn't you get?" he called into the mouthpiece. "The Inn is loaded with tourists at this time of year." And in three days, it would be at capacity. "It isn't a possibility."

"Yes," Denise argued, "it is, *if* you'll hear me out. I spoke to the manager and he said there are cabins onsite. They're being renovated, but they're habitable."

"Too hard to secure," Cody argued.

"We've faced worse situations," Denise reminded him. "Cody, think about it. We're light one deputy, and you've got to be at the Mountainview Inn for the reception for most of Saturday. If we use the cabins, you'd be close in case Martin or I need you."

Valid point. Dangerous, but valid. "I'll consider it. Where are you now?"

"I've got one more place on the list your brother gave me. It's a motel up toward Helena."

"Call Martin and have him scout it. It's on his way back from the lab. Tell him to call me. You get back here."

"Will do. But it might take me a little while. The roads are getting slick."

"Be careful."

"Always am."

Flipping the phone closed, Cody rubbed the stubble on his chin, considering all the possibilities presented by Denise's suggestion. There were some definite advantages to the Inn. He'd be able to attend to his family obligations without having to drive all over creation. Room service, he added to his mental notes as he pulled the pot of leftover stew from the fridge. He placed it on top of the stove and turned the knob that brought the flame to life on a sudden, blue-hot *whoosh,* then he turned it back to a low simmer.

The accommodations at the Inn could comfortably fit them all. A significant plus over this place, he decided as he glanced around the confined space. He went to the sofa and sat down. With his elbows on his knees, he steepled his fingers against his forehead and stared down at the tattered rug at his feet. Thankfully the smell of the warming stew was replacing the musty odor in the cabin. Nothing seemed to be able to replace his sense of normalcy.

After checking his watch, he put his cell phone and wallet on the coffee table then decided on a quick shower.

He stole one last glance at the closed bedroom door. She'd been in there for a few minutes. Remembering the escape she'd staged, he wondered—just for a second— if she'd done it again.

"No," he whispered, shaking his head as he flicked a switch to flood the cramped bath with harsh light from the single bulb in the center of the ceiling. "She wouldn't dare."

Would she? No. Not now. They had rapport, right?
A rapport that included a serious case of the hots.

Cody stripped and stepped under the spray of tepid water, replaying the scene back at the Lucky 7, followed by the passionate exchange in the living room. It didn't require closing his eyes to remember how great it had felt to have J.J. press her incredible body against him.

"I'm in serious trouble," he grumbled, lathering shampoo into his hair.

Yes, he lusted for her. But there was more. More than just a physical attraction. More than just a passing interest. More of everything. *How in the hell had this happened?*

It had to be lust. But some sort of mind-altering lust. A guy did *not* fall for a woman in less than ten days. *Right?*

He sighed. "Wrong." Worse than wrong.

And once J.J. found out the truth, she'd be furious. Beyond furious.

J.J. WAS FEELING smug, and a little bit naughty. Okay, a *lot* naughty. But who cared? Her body positively tingled from head to toe. She felt—what?

Happy. Really, really happy. Odd, considering that she was stuck in the middle of Montana. With a protective detail to keep the Russian mob from killing her. When said mob had tried twice already to do just that. With the help of one member of the detail. She should be on high alert. She should be doing her job. Not playing sex games.

Grabbing a small spoon from a sparsely stocked drawer, she tasted the stew, then lowered the burner.

She set the table. Admired her work. Then realized she had only put out two place settings. This only-the-two-of-us thing with Cody was as temporary as it was confusing, she reminded herself as she hastily grabbed place settings for Martin and Denise. She kept busy, secretly glad she didn't have time to explore her feelings. Forget explore. Acknowledge was a better word, but that, too, could wait. She saw movement out of the corner of her eye.

Crouched, she pulled her gun from the back of her waistband and considered yelling for Cody. No. Whoever was out there would hear her and, because of the shower, Cody would not.

She hadn't heard a car to signal Denise's or Martin's return. And, more suspiciously, whoever it was had flattened himself along the exterior of the cabin.

She took a series of deep breaths and counted… One…Two…Three. Then she yanked open the door and pointed the barrel of her gun even with the intruder's left temple. "Agent Barnes. FBI. Keep your hands where I can see them."

"Agent Neal Stephenson. Get your gun out of my face."

There was something vaguely familiar about the man. "Identification?"

"Left front pocket. Can we move this along? I know Landry is in the shower and the other two marshals will be back any minute. I've got a message for you from Associate Director Andrews and I'd like to give it to you before my lips freeze off."

"What are you doing here?" She kept the gun in place until she had verified his credentials.

Stephenson was about an inch shorter than her. A navy knit cap, crusted with snow, covered all but a hint of reddish-brown hair. Even in a bulky parka, he didn't appear to be muscular, but he certainly seemed annoyed enough to cause her pain if he felt so inclined. His blue eyes regarded her with unabashed irritation.

"Why here?" she insisted.

"Trying to get a message to you has been a little impossible. I've been buried under a snow mound for the better part of an hour."

After checking to make sure the shower was still running, she pulled him inside and closed the door. Whispering, she reminded him of the rules set up by the associate director. "Text message me, Stephenson. That's the plan."

"That *was* the plan," he groused. "Until someone reprogrammed your phone."

She blinked. "Someone…" It didn't take a stroke of genius to figure out who the culprit was.

"After walking nearly two miles in the snow, I had to wait to catch you alone. Look at this," Stephenson said, shoving a small digital camera in her direction. "I took this earlier today and sent a copy to your cell. Which—" he gave a judgmental little pause "—you didn't respond to. Mean anything to you?"

She shook her head. "That's Denise Howard." Wait? Was Stephenson watching? *Everything?* Lord, she hoped not.

As soon as he shut off the water, he heard something. His mind and heart raced. How could he have been so stupid as to leave J.J. alone?

After securing a towel around his waist and rifling through the pile of his discarded clothing, he grabbed his gun and soundlessly crept toward the closed door. Placing his ear against the roughly sanded wood, he isolated the muffled sounds of hushed voices. J.J.'s and— he strained to hear—a man?

Without hesitation, he reared back and kicked down the door, planting his feet and training his weapon dead center in the forehead of the startled guy standing in the entranceway.

J.J. rolled her eyes and placed her hands on her hips. "Stand down, Super Deputy," she mocked. "This is Agent Neal Stephenson." She walked over and put her hand on the barrel of his gun, applying pressure until he finally let it drop to his side.

"Stephenson, meet Deputy-Marshal-in-Charge Cody Landry."

"Landry," Stephenson said, standing rigidly and nodding in greeting.

J.J. watched the two men size each other up and felt the tide of testosterone lapping at her feet.

"Want to tell me what's going on here?" Cody snapped, directing his question at her.

The man had ears like a bat, J.J. thought. She and Stephenson had practically been lip reading. Damn. "Stephenson's my bureau shadow."

Cody's hostility seemed to fill the room. "And you were planning on telling me this *when?*"

"His existence was on a need-to-know basis. Until this moment, you didn't need to know." She met his angry gaze without flinching. "I knew I had a shadow, but not who until—"

"Third stool from the cash register at the Cowboy Café the night you escaped," Cody finished.

Okay, I'm impressed. "Very good." If she expected her compliment to diffuse some of the tension, she was wrong. Although he hadn't moved from his position in the bathroom doorway, every line of his body was taut and ready for action. *And* he was virtually *naked.*

Lust was clouding her judgment. "You had to know the bureau would make contact with me somehow."

He was beautiful, sculpted muscle. *Breathe. Don't think about the body. Don't think about the body.*

Not a muscle in his face or body relaxed. "I assumed the contact would go through proper channels."

Stephenson, sensing the undercurrents, smiled and tried to make light of a volatile situation. "You know what they say about assuming?"

His attempt at a joke hung in the air like a toxic cloud.

"Maybe you'd better go," J.J. suggested to Stephenson.

"But I'm supposed to brief—"

J.J. held up her hand. While she appreciated Stephenson's enthusiasm, she knew Cody well enough to know he wouldn't take what Stephenson was about to divulge well. She also didn't want Stephenson to pick up on the sexual undercurrents between herself and Cody. He'd report it in a heartbeat, and Associate Director Andrews was already seriously furious with her.

"Thanks for the info, Stephenson. I'll brief Deputy Landry," J.J. insisted as she ushered the agent out the door.

After seeing the agent off on his long walk back to wherever, she turned her gaze back on Cody. "Stephenson came here to do more than just brief me. He ratted you out about the cell phone."

"Really?" he asked, arching one dark brow.

Damp, dark hair covered his broad chest and narrowed toward his trim waist and taut abdomen. *Eyes up. Don't think about the body.*

Six feet, four inches of acutely annoyed, practically naked deputy marshal glowered in her direction.

"Don't you dare look at me like that," she shot at him. "Exactly when were *you* going to tell *me* the truth?"

"You were on a need-to-know basis." He repeated what she'd told him minutes ago, his words still clipped by anger. "You didn't need to know."

"I've been totally up-front with you, Cody. I put myself out there—all cards on the table—only to discover you've been screwing with me this whole time."

"Nothing personal, Agent Barnes." Cody strode to the stove to turn off the stew. He turned back around to look at her, his eyes cool. "We were both doing our jobs."

Yes, they were. Then why, J.J. wondered, did his betrayal hurt this much? "Did you think the FBI wouldn't put a tracking device in my cell phone? Not only does it have a GPS function, but the FBI can access my text messages. They know what you did. And now I know."

"Sorry, J.J., but you're the one who broke the rules first."

"What?"

"It took me about ten seconds to find your cell phone," he said flatly. "Less time to hack in. You were the one who accepted the alternate contact address I sent without bothering to confirm the change through a separate channel."

"That's your excuse for rerouting my text messages? You made me look bad, Cody. That was a lousy thing to do."

"A *lousy* thing to do?" He scrubbed his jaw. "Listen to yourself. This isn't a frigging company picnic, J.J. Seriously bad people are determined to kill you. I was doing my job. And my job is to keep you alive until you have to testify. By whatever means I have at my disposal. Anyone on this team, including you, who made contact beyond the five of us was subject to scrutiny.

"The fact that you were stupid enough to be texting messages to *anybody* required that I keep track of to whom and about what." He reached her in two strides. "Want to talk about unprofessional? How about you bringing a cell phone and a gun when you were specifically told not to."

"I had good reason." Raising her chin proudly, J.J. held his gaze. "Besides…that was before."

"Before what?" He moved closer.

He watched transfixed as she swallowed and her lips

parted but no sound emerged. Great lips. Rosy and full. Completely kissable.

"Before what?" he pressed, moving one palm to her waist.

"J-just *before.*"

Her tone was hard to decipher. Was she still mad? Or was she feeling the same strong draw that had him wanting to kiss her senseless?

She shoved away from him and ran to get her cell phone. "Who is this?" She showed him the grainy photograph Stephenson had forwarded. It showed today's date and Denise standing next to the SUV exchanging a manila envelope with a well-dressed man.

"I have no clue," Cody stated through tightly clenched teeth.

"Stephenson got the license plate. They're running it now."

"Give me a minute to throw on some clothes." Cody marched to the bedroom. She heard him curse after slamming the door so forcefully that the whole cabin rattled.

J.J. winced. "He took that well."

She went to the sofa to wait. As soon as she was seated, the cell phone on the coffee table began to vibrate. She knew it was Cody's, but that didn't stop her from reading the display.

Martin—9-1-1.

Grabbing the phone, she pressed a button and said, "Yes?"

"H-help me."

Chapter Eleven

"No indication of where he was calling from?" Cody asked. Concerned, he shoved one arm and then the other into his jacket sleeves en route to the door. "Stew…"

"I've got it." J.J. jogged back to turn off the stove half in, half out of her coat. She finished shrugging into it as she followed him outside. "The line is still open. Can your brother help us?"

He called out the number to Seth's direct line as they headed to the Hummer through a snowstorm. Denise had been right. Efficiently J.J. dialed Seth, explained the situation, then told him what they needed, pausing only to ask Cody for Martin's number so the sheriff's office could use it to triangulate the active signal.

Driving was difficult. Snow swirled in every direction, creating a nearly consuming cloud of white flakes that enveloped the car and all but a few feet of the road ahead. Inching along only added to Cody's sense of concern and frustration.

Assuming Martin had been heading *back* from Helena when the emergency happened, Cody steered toward town, where he could easily pick up the interstate.

It wasn't necessary. They were maybe three-quarters of a mile from the cabin when they spotted the Marshal Service's SUV on the side of the road and a blue sedan in a ditch, almost obscured by snow and the dense clump of trees. Denise was in the ditch, jumping up and down, frantically waving her gloved hands.

Because of the snowdrift, Cody had to park the Hummer with part of the vehicle still in the roadway. Jumping out of the car, he skidded over to Denise with J.J. right on his heels.

Martin was sitting in the ravine holding his scarf against the side of his head. The snow around him was stained red with blood.

"What happened?" Cody demanded as he slid down the embankment to reach Martin. Without glancing at Denise, he asked, "Did you call it in?"

"Ambulance on the way," she confirmed.

J.J. crouched next to Martin, peeling back the scarf so they could examine the injury.

"You'll live," Cody said, relieved.

"We have tracks," J.J. said, reaching out to grip Cody's forearm.

Following her line of sight, he saw the fast-disappearing ruts that headed to the road and to the clump of trees. "Too trampled to do much good."

"One set is mine," Denise explained. "I wanted to make sure our perp wasn't laying in wait. Found remnants of a small fire beyond the trees and another set of footprints doubling back toward town."

Cody watched as J.J. stood and surveyed the scene, her hand shielding her eyes from the swirling snow. He could almost read her thoughts.

"Why would he risk walking back and forth enough times to make a trench in the snow? And how could the perp have known to wait in *those* trees for Martin?"

"Ice patch," Martin explained, hooking his thumb over his shoulder. "All I know is I started a skid, ended up in a ditch and when I got out of the car, someone cleaned my clock but good."

Cody and J.J. climbed back up the embankment and walked onto the road. Sure enough, with the toe of his boot he found a layer of ice hidden beneath the inch and a half of freshly fallen snow. Using his gloves, he swept the powdery flakes away to reveal a frozen strip. "This isn't a natural patch of black ice."

"No kidding," J.J. commented, her brow deeply furrowed as she glanced around. "We need forensics on this. How many gallons of water would it have taken to rig the skid and—"

"Come on," Cody interrupted, then pointed toward the trees. The snow continued to fall in earnest as they ran toward the heavy scent of pine mixed with the familiar smell of wood smoke.

As the wail of a distant siren split through the silence, Cody ducked beneath low branches, following the pungent smell, until he found the makeshift campsite.

"This guy knew what he was doing," Cody explained when J.J. appeared a second behind him. Squatting back on his heels, he used a partially charred twig to point as he spoke. "The rut happened as he melted snow." He pointed toward a patch of snowless ground near the fire. "He used the snowmelt to make the ice patch on the roadway."

"And carried it in what?" J.J. asked.

Cody surveyed the area until he found a possible answer among the trash littered about. Reaching behind a tree trunk, he retrieved a bright red gas can. "I'm guessing this."

"Doesn't appear to have been out here long," she observed. "No rust or dust. And hard to trace."

He agreed. "It's too generic, but maybe our perp left some prints."

"Maybe," she agreed, though he didn't hear a lot of conviction in her words. "Ambulance is here."

Red and white strobe lights decorated the snow as the E.M.T.s loaded Martin—who was protesting loudly—into the ambulance and whisked him off to the hospital.

Seth pulled up his Jeep and placed bright orange, reflective traffic cones around the site. Then he directed a tow truck driver to winch the sedan out of the ditch.

"Denise, go back and secure the cabin." Cody had to yell to be heard above the monotonous warning beeps made by the truck as it moved into position. Turning to his brother, he said, "Let's get in the Hummer. I don't like having J.J. out here in the open so long."

"I know, it doesn't feel right." Seth's expression probably mirrored his own.

J.J. climbed into the passenger seat while Seth hoisted himself into the back. Cody slid behind the wheel, started the engine and blasted heat into the compartment. He ticked off the items he wanted preserved and collected as evidence.

J.J. thought for a minute before putting her two cents in. "Denise could have staged the whole thing."

Cody shot her a withering look. Seth remained silent.

"Well," J.J. argued, "it would account for her long absence today and the photograph Neal brought us. Maybe the envelope she was handing the guy was payment for setting up Martin's 'accident.'"

"No motive," Cody stated.

"Want to fill me in?" Seth asked, diffusing some of the tension in the air.

Cody explained about the fire, the ice patch, the gas can and their theory on how Martin was ambushed.

"Creative," Seth remarked, rubbing his chin before shoving the Stetson farther back on his head. "You think it was Denise?"

"Yes," J.J. said.

"No," Cody said.

The debate had to wait because the tow truck driver tapped on the window. "Found something you might want to see."

J.J. followed the Landry brothers out into the blustery cold. A biting wind whipped the snow around in a series of flaky white tornadoes that made it hard to see much farther than a foot in front of her. The short walk took some doing, since the footing was dicey.

She started to slip and would have landed squarely on her tailbone had Cody not grabbed her arm and saved her from that humiliation. His strength was admirable.

She was no lightweight and it was no small feat to keep her upright. "Thanks."

"Hold on to me," he suggested.

She did. Just touching him was enough to transform her from capable FBI agent into quivering, needy Hormone Girl. Instead of focusing on whatever the tow truck guy wanted them to see, she could only think of the fact that her fingertips fell well short of meeting as she encircled his impressive bicep. With each cautious step, their bodies brushed. No amount of layers could prevent her from feeling the electricity where they touched.

When they reached the edge of the roadway, she had to force herself to let go. Chilled and struggling to see through the haze of snowflakes, J.J. adjusted her scarf as she bent down to join the semicircle of men examining the object.

A blood-spattered baseball bat lay in the snow where the car had been. "Why leave the weapon here?" J.J. wondered aloud.

"Because walking down the road with a bloody club might attract attention?" Cody suggested.

"We need to talk to Martin," she decided. "There's something wrong about this."

"I agree," Seth stated.

"We'll handle it," Cody said, sending a *you're-a-traitor* look his brother's way. He held out his hand to her.

J.J. gladly accepted. It took twice the time it should have to work their way back to the Hummer.

"Maybe we should wait until the conditions improve," she suggested, shaking snow from her boots and clothing before climbing into the warmth of the waiting vehicle.

"This is Montana," he replied dryly. "Conditions don't improve until spring."

"Okay, then." She buckled in for what she was sure would be a tricky ride.

Cody made it seem easy. He anticipated when to ease off the gas and how to manipulate the wheel to keep the Hummer in the lane. He could have hogged the road, because there weren't any other cars between the accident site and the hospital.

"You made that seem like a cakewalk."

"Practice," he told her as he parked in the lot marked Physicians Only and cut the engine.

"This is illegal."

Flashing a killer grin, he said, "Not really. This vehicle belongs to the ranch. Chance has an interest in the ranch. Ergo, this is Chance's gas guzzling monster."

"You went a long way to justify that one, Landry," she joked before preparing to step out into what she would classify as a blizzard.

"Why do you call me Landry all the time?" he asked when they reached the hospital's automatic door.

It opened on a release of air and her lungs filled with the antiseptic smell of the place. Muffled voices, crying children and static from the intercom system all converged at once. The place was mobbed. No matter how experienced a driver was, in this kind of weather accidents happened.

"Habit, probably," she admitted.

"I'm a habit now?" he joked, winking as they walked and shed layers of coats, gloves and scarves.

"Work habit," she clarified, using her fingers to try to fluff some volume into her hair. A wasted effort. Catching her reflection in the metal doors ahead, she admitted she had a serious case of hat hair. Her cheeks were red and raw from the cold, which only highlighted the yellowish taint of the bruise still on her right cheek. "Do deputy marshals call each other by their first names?"

"Yes. I guess we aren't as anal as the feebs."

"We aren't anal, we're professionals," she joked.

He stopped at the nursing station and, thanks to a gushing, buxom brunette, they learned that Martin was in X-ray and would be given a room shortly.

Spying a row of upholstered chairs, Cody led her to them. Piling their coats on the seat next to them, he stretched out his long legs, then crossed them at the ankles.

"So, why J.J.? I think Juliette is a pretty name."

She cringed. "Juliette is a prom queen name and I was never big on tiaras. Did you read that in my file?"

"Yep."

"Not very interesting reading. You must've been bored. What else were you privy to?"

He shrugged and closed his eyes, leaning his dark head against the smoothly tiled wall. "Juliette Joanna Barnes. Born June 3, 1969, in Marietta, Georgia, to Ester and Jacob Barnes. Attended John F. Kennedy Elementary School where you were a straight A student with a penchant for activism."

J.J. grinned at the memory. "My school—in complete violation of Title IX— would not allow me to play on the boys' basketball team even though they didn't have a girls' team."

"And you showed them," he teased. "But don't you think writing an amicus brief to the Supreme Court at the age of nine was a little excessive?"

"It seemed like a good idea at the time. Too bad I didn't know there had to be a case before the court before you could file a brief. But it made the papers *and* the point."

"Yeah." He sighed loudly. "Your school put you on the team, but the coach only let you play a total of seven minutes all season."

"But I played."

"Won the battle and lost the war, if you ask me."

"Easy for you to say. You're a man. You have no clue what it's like to have to prove yourself every inch of every step of the way. Especially if you happen to take a path that is outside the comfort zone of traditional expectation."

"That explains your activities in high school. As I recall—" he peeked at her from the corner of one eye, his mouth twitching with amusement "—you demanded the school board remove any gender-specific references from standardized testing."

"Which was done."

"Five years after you graduated." He chuckled. "Hardly helpful to you."

"But helpful to others," she said tartly. "Sometimes change takes time."

"Sometimes change is pointless. Does it change the answer to a word problem by neutralizing all the pronouns? You still have to do the algebra to figure out when the train will arrive in Newark even if it is, thanks to you, loaded with hermaphrodites."

"You're mocking me, Landry." Before she realized what she was doing, she found herself reaching up and brushing the dark hair off his forehead.

The busy hospital setting evaporated and it seemed as if they were the only people on the planet. Her ears no longer heard anything but his even breathing. She smelled nothing but his faint cologne. She saw only him.

"This is getting to be a problem, isn't it?" he asked in a near whisper that managed to set her heart pounding.

"Mmm-hmm."

He reached out and cupped her cheek in his warm palm. Reflexively she leaned into it, resting her head in the cradle of his touch.

"Half of my team is here in the hospital and all I can think about is kissing you."

A thrill danced the length of her spine. "It's good to have priorities."

The pad of his thumb went to her lower lip, applying sweet pleasure that sent sparks through her system. His eyes lowered, following the movement of his thumb. She watched as his pupils became pinpoints and his mouth drew into a tight, purposeful line.

"We need to get—"

"A room," Dr. Chance Landry announced cheerfully as he joined them.

J.J. flew bolt upright. She felt her face warm with a blush as she did her best to offer the doctor a guilt-tainted smile.

Chance didn't seem the least bit fazed at catching them in such an intimate breech of professional decorum. Nor, she noted with more than just a bit of envy and annoyance, did Cody.

"You paying?" Cody teased, shifting the coats so his brother could join them.

"No. And neither are you. She's on the Do Not Disturb list, dear bro."

"*She* is sitting right here," J.J. tersely reminded both of them. *Did everyone have to know her personal business? And did they have to chat about it like they were discussing the flaming weather?*

"Sorry, J.J., how are you feeling?"

Humiliated. "Great."

"No complications?"

"No." She planted a saccharine smile on her face. "No doctor-patient confidentiality, either."

Chance cocked his head and tried to look repentant. "Should I pretend that Cody hasn't peppered me with questions he would only know to ask if you'd confided in him?"

"Um…yes."

He laughed. "I'll make you a deal. You come to my office in the next couple of days for that follow-up and I'll forgive you for not keeping in contact like you promised."

"There's nothing to follow up," she argued. "I feel perfectly fine. Completely back to normal."

"That's the problem," Chance said, his tone suddenly more serious. "You may feel fine and have no residual symptoms, but you aren't fine yet." He turned to Cody and added, "And my brother should keep that in mind at all times."

Cody raised his hands in mock surrender. "I get it, I get it. Move along, you're making her blush."

Oh, she was beyond mere blush. She was definitely ready for the floor to open and swallow her whole.

Chance flipped open the metal file and thumbed efficiently through the quarter inch of pages. "Martin's gash didn't need sutures."

"Stitches." Cody groaned, turning to her in order to add, "He only uses those words because he likes to think he's smarter than the rest of us."

"I am." Chance sighed heavily. "I got all the brains in the family. But back to Martin, he's got a concussion and I'm keeping him overnight because of the loss of consciousness."

"He blacked out?" J.J. questioned.

Chance nodded and read from the notes, "Patient reports brief period of unconsciousness lasting less than five minutes in duration." He closed the chart. "He's alert and responsive, so it really is just a precautionary measure."

"Can we talk to him?" Cody asked.

"Sure. I'm having him put in the room next to Deputy Selznick." In a brotherly dig, he added, "I'll keep two more rooms open on that floor in case the rest of your detail needs a place to mend."

"Kiss my—"

"This is a public place, Cody," Chance warned. "See you tomorrow at the day-before-the-wedding breakfast?"

"Maybe," Cody hedged. It earned him a stern look

from his brother. "What am I supposed to do? Leave J.J. with Den—leave her insufficiently protected?"

"Bring her along," Chance suggested. "It's adult only at the house. Chandler's orders. Seth should be able to arrange to secure the ranch for a few hours."

"I wouldn't want to impose," J.J. injected, terrified at the prospect of entering Landry Land. There was something really he's-my-boyfriend about that.

He wasn't her boyfriend. He was more like her... what? The line between protector and protectee had been so blurred that it no longer existed. And she'd also erased him as a suspect. If the FBI knew that, she'd sure lose her job because, God knew, her conclusion wasn't based on any tangible fact. No, she'd excluded him on instinct alone.

"We'd love to have you," Chance insisted. "Especially since it will prevent Cody from having an excuse to leave when the rest of us are trapped in Wedding Hell with no way out. I was going to arrange to have myself paged until Val threatened me with bodily harm if I didn't cooperate."

"As well you should," J.J. insisted. "But it's a family thing and I'm—"

"Going," Cody announced, taking her by the hand and urging her to her feet. "Third floor?" he asked his brother.

"Yep. See you in the morning, J.J.," Chance called.

"I really don't think it's appropriate for me to go to a family function," she argued as Cody pressed the elevator call button.

"It's my family, J.J., not a firing squad," he teased. "Besides, the alternative is to leave you with Denise."

She arched one brow as she examined his unreadable expression. "You think she…that she's the leak?"

He sucked in a deep breath and let it out slowly. Then, with obvious and pained reluctance, he asked, "Are you telling me that whole scene back there made sense to you?"

Chapter Twelve

The elevator doors slid open, revealing an almost deserted corridor. A low humming sound came from the buffing machine being used by an elderly janitor as he rocked it back and forth across the floor. Two nurses worked at the L-shaped desk. Behind them was a dry erase board with the names of all the patients on the floor.

Furious, Cody pressed the winter gear in J.J.'s general direction. "Hold these." He marched over, grabbed one of the nurse's sweaters off the back of a chair, and began rubbing two names off the board.

"Hey!" the older of the two snapped.

Turning, he glared down at the woman, angrier than hell. "Martin Newell's name does not belong up here. Lara Selznick's name does not belong up here." Reaching into his pocket, he flipped out his badge and wagged it in the stunned faces of the women.

"Sorry," they each muttered in turn.

Glancing down at the sweater, Cody felt a pang of guilt and realized his spurt of anger was not only because listing the names of his team placed them in jeopardy. He was worried. Worried that J.J. was right. It was possible—just *possible*—that she'd been right all along. Someone on the inside had flipped. Someone he trusted.

"Have this cleaned or replaced and send the bill to me." Tossing the garment back on the chair, he strode back to J.J. and took the coats from her before heading down the hallway.

"You did that out of sequence," J.J. suggested with annoying reason. "You could have shown them your ID, then explained why having the names on that board was dangerous."

"Could have, possibly should have. But that would've taken too long."

J.J. stopped suddenly and yanked him inside the empty room adjacent to Lara's, closing the door. Grabbing the coats from him, she tossed them on a cardboard box labeled Steri-Strips. She tilted her head back and looked at him with intense scrutiny.

"What?" he snapped, when a few seconds passed without her saying a word.

"All of a sudden, you're wound up like the proverbial top. What's the problem?"

"The problem," he said tightly, "is that someone I know, possibly someone I work with and trust, might very well be involved in getting other people I know and trust killed. You being a primary target."

"Nobody's going to kill me," J.J. insisted. "I've got you and I've got me. I like those odds. I'm sure this is hard for you, Cody, but keep it in perspective. Those nurses back there weren't the enemy."

"We can't say who the enemy is, can we?"

She offered a soft smile and placed her palms against

his chest. "We make a good team, Cody. All we have to do is go back to the basics."

"Means, motive and opportunity," he recited by rote. Taking one of her hands, he led her over to the bed and pulled her down to sit with him on the edge, careful not to topple the supplies stacked all around them. Apparently the hospital was in dire need of storage space since they'd turned a perfectly good patient room into a closet.

"Let's start with Lara," she suggested. "Tell me about her."

"Lara? She's the least likely person, don't you think? Yes, she's the newest member of my team, but there's no motivation that we can tell at this point. Besides, she got blown up…at the…" J.J. twisted her hair up into a knot, distracting him for a moment. He regrouped. "At Simms farm."

If she only knew how he wanted to pull the knot loose and run his fingers through the silky strands. Or if she'd realized that by raising her arms to tame her hair, her full, round breasts pressed a vivid outline against the soft, beige sweater.

"Stop thinking dirty thoughts, Landry," she said with a smile that softened the verbal spanking.

Guess she did.

"Can't help it," he admitted, tapping the tip of her nose with his finger. "You're quite the distraction, Agent Barnes."

"As are you," she admitted freely, trapping his finger and bringing it to her mouth.

Cody's eyes glazed. "Do you say things like that to me because you know I can't do anything about them?"

She returned his hand to the taut sheet between them with a little pat. The grin she managed was a little on the sheepish side, but the smoldering in her eyes raised his pulse rate several notches. "Probably."

He blew out an exasperated breath. "One day soon, Chance is going to give you the all clear and I'm not going to have the self-control of a statue. Remember that."

Remember it? She was tingling all over just hearing it! "I'll be sure to mark it in my week-at-a-glance," she teased. "Back to Lara." *So I stop thinking about the fact that your thigh is pressing against mine.*

He was stroking his chin, and she could almost see the cogs in his brain turning. Finally he said, "She's young. Prickly."

"Prickly?"

His eyes narrowed. "Are you going to critique my adjectives, or may I continue?"

"Sorry. Feel free."

"Lara hasn't really meshed with the group," he explained. "She has a habit of purposefully segregating herself. I figured it was because we've all been together for a while and she's the newbie. That can be intimidating."

"I sensed something hinky."

He chuckled softly. "You ragged me for saying 'prickly' but you get to use 'hinky' in a sentence?"

"Pretty much," she assured him sweetly. "She's smart, Cody. Really, really smart."

"You gave her an IQ test?"

She shook her head. "While you were off in Landry Land, I watched her whip through word search puzzles. She's amazing."

"Athletic, too," he added. "So it really doesn't make sense for a smart, athletic woman to blow herself up, does it?"

J.J. had to give him that one. "Unless something went awry with the planning." She told him how Martin and Lara had argued over the snowmobile that had exploded. "But that doesn't make sense, either, because it wasn't like we planned to go out for a ride. And Lara was absolutely dead set against going."

"I'm not crossing anyone off the list, including Lara. Not until we find out what she may be hiding."

"I'm pretty partial to the direct approach," J.J. replied.

"It can be effective."

"Then let's directly discuss Denise," J.J. prompted. "I know you have your suspicions. That's why you roped me into the family thing, right?"

"You're the one who showed me the photo," Cody returned. "She met someone. She's the only member of the team who hasn't been injured."

"Except you."

He cast her a look that was part annoyance and part open wound. "Am I still on your list, J.J.?"

Patting the back of his hand again, she met his eyes and said, "No."

"She's also one of the last people I'd ever dream would put a protectee in danger. Setting aside the fact that I've known her for years and worked with her for the last five, she takes her job very seriously. She's devoted. She chose the job over a family. Is just doesn't fit."

"Maybe something has changed," J.J. suggested carefully. She stood to pace the small confines of the room. "What if something has happened in her life? Something serious enough for her to turn."

Cody dropped his head into his hands, and J.J. battled a strong urge to comfort him. This was an emotional issue he'd have to work through himself.

When he looked up again, his eyes were narrowed in thought. "Denise had the opportunity," he admitted. "Means is easy. Her father was a demo expert in the Army. But motive? I just can't see it."

"Her father was a demo expert?" J.J. felt a surge of anger. "Were you planning on sharing that fact with me anytime soon?"

"It didn't seem relevant."

She threw her hands in the air, then let them slap down loudly. "A snowmobile is remote detonated and you didn't think Denise having a history with explosives was relevant?"

"*She* doesn't have a history," Cody responded. "Her father does. Did. He died several years ago. C'mon, J.J., can you do whatever it was your father did?"

"I sure can," she shot back. "Just as I'm sure you can do cows."

He glared at her for an instant, then started laughing. *"Do cows?"*

"Forgive me for not paying closer attention to *Bonanza* reruns, hoss. I'm not up to speed on ranching terms. But my point remains the same. Even though you chose another path, I'll bet you know…ranch things."

"Enough to know I don't like it," he promised her, his lips still curved in a far too annoying grin. "And don't think I'm impressed that you learned your father's trade. He made hats, as I recall."

"The term is milliner," she informed him in her haughtiest tone. "His designs were works of art. Southern women used to appreciate a good hat. My father made a decent living, thank you very much. Not up to par with Landry standards, but we got by just fine until ready-made replaced custom-made. So just—"

"Chill," he interrupted, still grinning. "I wasn't maligning the hat industry. I am *chapeau* sorry."

She smacked his arm with a little more force than necessary. *Hats? I'm arguing with him about hats? I don't even like hats!* "Bad hat reference notwithstanding, apology accepted. Sorry for getting so worked up. I guess it's just tension…."

He reached for her. "I'm ready to kiss and make up."

She slapped away his outstretched hand. "Something tells me you're perpetually ready to kiss and make up."

"Do you mean…dare I say it? At the drop of a hat?" His smile faded as he reached for her again. "By the way, no. Not usually."

His lips brushed against the sensitive skin just below her earlobe. The feel of his feather-light kisses drew her stomach into a knot of anticipation. Closing her eyes, she concentrated on the glorious sensations.

His grip on her tightened as his tongue traced a path up to her ear. Her breath caught when he teasingly nibbled the edge of her lobe. His hands traveled upward and rested against her rib cage. She swallowed the moan rumbling in her throat. She was aware of everything—

his fingers; the feel of his solid body molded against hers; the magical kisses.

"You smell wonderful," he said against her heated skin.

"Cody," she whispered. "I don't think this is such a good idea."

His mouth stilled. His dark eyes were hooded. A lock of his jet-black hair had fallen forward and rested just above his brows. His chiseled mouth was curved in an effortlessly sexy half-smile as he applied pressure to the middle of her back, urging her closer to him.

"We shouldn't do this," she managed above her rapid heartbeat.

"I know," he agreed, punctuating his remark with a kiss on her forehead. "Problem is, I look at you and I can't think of anything *but* this."

His palms slid up her back until he cradled her face in his hands. Using his thumbs, he tilted her head back and hesitated only fractionally before his mouth found hers. Instinctively J.J.'s hands went to his waist. She could feel the tapered muscles stiffen in response to her touch.

The scent of soap and cologne filled her senses as the exquisite pressure of his mouth increased. His hands left her face and began to massage their way toward her spine, his fingertips slowly, sensuously counting each vertebra. Her mind was no longer capable of rational thought.

She began to explore the solid contours of his body beneath his soft cotton shirt. It was like feeling the smooth, sculpted surface of granite. Everywhere she touched she felt the distinct outline of corded muscle. She could even feel the vibration from his erratic pulse.

When he broke the kiss, she had to fight to keep from giving in to her strong urge to pull him back to her. His eyes searched her face. His breaths were coming in short, almost raspy gulps and she watched the tiny vein at his temple race in time with her own rapid heartbeat.

"I've never done this," he said.

J.J.'s eyes opened wider and her expression must have conveyed her obvious shock.

Cody's chuckle was deep and reached his eyes.

"I've done *it*," he corrected. "I've just never had to be so completely restrained before."

"How's it working out for you?"

"Not that well," he said as he claimed her mouth again. His kiss lasted for several heavenly moments. "As much as I love the way your mouth feels, I'm thinking it's really hard to do nothing but kiss you."

"I don't think I *am* thinking," she admitted as she rested her cheek against his throat.

"Maybe I don't want us to think, J.J."

"That isn't very responsible behavior," she said against the soft fabric covering his broad chest.

"I can't tell you how responsibly I've been taking my cold showers lately." He hooked his thumb under her chin and forced her to meet his eyes. She tried to ignore the sudden tightness in the pit of her stomach.

"Cody, I think—"

She didn't finish her thought. A raised voice in the room next door suddenly had their complete attention.

Chapter Thirteen

Like two conspirators, Cody and J.J. placed their ears to the wall and listened to the snippets of harsh, one-sided conversation.

J.J. was having trouble hearing it all. Not because Lara's voice didn't carry, but because her heartbeat was still pounding in her ears. Her legs weren't all that steady, either. A Cody Landry kiss had the power to melt bone.

"This is ridiculous," Cody grumbled, taking her hand and pulling her toward the door.

"Hang on," J.J. insisted, stopping him. "Let me go in alone."

"Why?"

"Because you're her boss. She might be more open with me. If I bomb, you can go in and do your thing."

"Good cop, bad cop?" he teased.

"More like girl cop, boy cop," she corrected, getting on tiptoe to plant a kiss on his lips. She patted his cheek. "Don't worry, Landry, she's got a broken collarbone and even if she didn't, I could still take her."

He made a production out of rubbing his back. "I remember."

"Wuss...ouch!" she yelped when his hand made solid contact with her rear end.

As she suspected, the second she entered Lara's room, the marshal slammed the telephone receiver back on its cradle. "Barnes?" she greeted nervously.

After calmly closing the door, J.J. moved into the sparse room and pulled one of the twin Naugahyde chairs close to the edge of the bed. Apparently foregoing the hospital issue gown, Lara was wearing a navy blue T-shirt with the Marshal Service's emblem on the breast pocket and a pair of shorts. Her left arm was in a sling and her short-cropped hair was a spiky, disorganized mess.

"How are you?" J.J. asked, sitting down.

"Ready to leave. How's Martin?"

"News travels fast, huh?"

"How is he?" Lara repeated, her expression as guarded as her tone.

"Concussion and a cut on his head. Cody is waiting for him to get settled in his room, so I thought I'd drop by and say hello. I'm glad to see you're doing okay and really glad that Martin wasn't more seriously hurt."

"How'd it happen?"

J.J. suspected that Lara knew exactly what had transpired. But she played along by retelling the story. "I'm sure he'll be in to visit as soon as they get him all settled in his room."

"Maybe. I'm glad he wasn't hurt. We don't need anyone else out of commission right now."

"True. But it will be nice for you to have some company, won't it?" J.J. asked.

"I'm not planning on staying that long. I was supposed to be out by now, but apparently Cody put a hold on my release."

Really? Another detail he forgot to mention. "I'm sure he's just thinking of what is in your best interest."

"Don't bet on it," Lara fairly sneered. "But he's in charge, so that's the way it goes. Like it or not."

"It's frustrating being sidelined," she commiserated. "After my surgery, I had nearly two months of inactivity. Made me crazy."

Lara seemed to relax a bit. "That was a tough break."

"Sure was. It's put a crimp in my career, too. It doesn't do much for one's self-confidence to realize no one trusts you."

"Forget trust, Barnes. I'm still working on respect."

"That took me some time," J.J. agreed, settling back into the chair. "I had to work twice as hard to get half the respect of my male counterparts."

"Which is total crap," Lara scoffed, rubbing her disheveled hair. "You didn't blow the Visnopov case."

"No. But once the U.S. Attorney executed the warrants, my cover was blown."

"They left you out in the field to get your ass kicked."

"I'm sure that wasn't part of the plan." J.J. wasn't feeding Lara a line; she really did believe that her beating was an unavoidably poor turn of events. "My boss knew how close I was to getting solid proof against Visnopov. We took every possible precaution. Including getting some of the key players into protective custody while I was still on the inside."

Lara's eyes narrowed and her hands balled into

tight fists. "We did everything possible to keep those guys safe."

"I know," J.J. insisted, hoping to diffuse Lara's defensiveness. "The Russians are good. We thought we'd covered our tracks before turning the witnesses over to you. The first witness...Basniak...we rigged it so it appeared he had a heart attack right in front of Visnopov's top lieutenant. We went so far as to have agents dressed as paramedics come and perform CPR. Thought it worked. Did similar stuff to extract the other two. Elaborate and fail-safe—or so we thought."

"I swear, Barnes, we did everything by the book." Lara's tone indicated only that she took the failures personally.

Either she was one hell of an actress, or she wasn't involved in getting the witnesses killed. Still, J.J.'s gut was insisting there was something going on with the young woman. How to get it out of her? There was always the direct approach. "So, who were you yelling at?"

Lara's eyes darted from the phone, to a pad on the bedside table, then back to J.J. "It was official business," she hedged. "Privileged, Barnes. You know the drill."

J.J. nodded and got to her feet. "I'll see what I can do about getting Cody to lift your sentence." *And get my hands on whatever is on that pad that you don't want me to see.*

"J.J. headed for the door.

"Barnes?"

There was something tentative in the way Lara had said her name. Thinking she might be ready to share something, J.J. didn't risk turning around and spooking her. "Yes?"

"Don't make it harder for the rest of us."

"Meaning?"

"Cody's already distracted by his family stuff. He needs to be sharp right now. That won't happen if he's sleeping with you."

J.J. took in a deep breath and exhaled slowly. "He isn't."

"Good. Keep it that way."

As if I have a choice.

"I NEVER SAW IT coming," Martin said, shaking his head and wincing from the action.

Lacing his fingers behind his head as he leaned back in the chair, Cody regarded his longtime friend and felt a certain amount of guilt well up inside of him. This was his operation and, to date, two of his deputies had been hospitalized. Not exactly a stellar record.

"Must have whacked the steering wheel when I spun into the ditch," Martin continued. "All I know is that when I opened the car door, wham! Whoever hit me had a helluva arm. I must have crawled out into the snow, 'cause that's the next clear memory I have."

"You didn't see anyone along the road?"

"Not before, during or after."

"Think back, Martin. Maybe you saw a shadow, anything that might give us a place to start?"

He shrugged and offered an embarrassed smile. "Sorry, my friend. The only clear image in my head is seeing those ugly fake fur boots Denise wears. But that was after I was hit, right? No help there."

Cody rose and patted his friend's shoulder. "Get some rest tonight. Lara is right next door."

Martin's brow furrowed. "I thought she was getting out today."

"I want her here to keep an eye on you."

"What about Barnes? Doesn't that leave you short?"

"May not be by the book, but I do have a whole posse of Landrys I can call into service if need be."

"Are you going back to the cabin?"

Cody shook his head. "Time to move again."

"Why?" Martin pressed. "Have you forgotten the purpose of this assignment? We're supposed to let them find her."

Cody felt physically ill as he headed out the door.

"…again, Miss, we don't straighten rooms. That's the job of the custodial staff." The nurse, whose sweater he'd used as an eraser, was talking with J.J. in the hallway in a particularly affronted tone.

"Problem?" he asked, moving to J.J.'s side and placing a hand at the small of her back.

J.J. glanced up at him and explained, "All I want her to do is take fresh water into Lara's room, pretend to be tidying up and replace the notepad on the table."

"Because?"

"Because there's something on that pad that made her pretty nervous."

Cody looked at the nurse and said, "Do it, please."

Nurse Nose-Out-of-Joint complied, gathering up a few props before her rubber-soled, bright-white shoes squished as she went on her assigned task.

Turning and resting his elbows against the desktop,

Cody replayed the conversation with Martin in his head. It was looking like Denise just might be a leak. As much as it pained him to believe it, the evidence—circumstantial to be sure—was mounting.

"Who kicked your dog?" J.J. challenged.

Glancing over, he saw fire in her aqua gaze. Probably not a good sign. "What's that supposed to mean?"

"It means—" J.J. leaned toward him, her eyes glistening "—that you've been keeping secrets, Landry."

His heart stopped. *She knew.* "I can explain."

"Start now," she insisted. "Explain why you arranged for Lara to stay in the hospital. If you were having doubts about her, explain why you didn't share them with me." She paused only long enough to rake her fingers through her hair. "Then explain to me why you didn't think you could trust me with your suspicions."

She didn't know.

Yet.

It was only a matter of time. That much was clear. Hopefully if they found the leak—even if it turned out to be one of his own—he'd never have to own up to being complicit in putting her in danger.

"It was a snap judgment," he defended. "With Martin and Lara here at the hospital, we can put the full court press on Denise."

She easily accepted his explanation and he wasn't sure if that was good or bad. He wasn't sure of a whole hell of a lot just now. He only knew that he had her trust, and had done nothing to earn it. Not a pretty place to be.

"Here," the nurse said on her return, slapping a blank pad on the counter. "Will there be anything else?"

"No," Cody answered for them both, swiping up the item and retrieving their coats before leading J.J. down to the doctor's lounge on the first floor.

As soon as they were inside the deserted lounge, J.J. grabbed the pad from him as if she was retrieving a prize.

"It's blank," he offered.

"Not a problem," she assured him as she went to the cluttered desk and grabbed a pencil. "A little game of Secret Code and we'll be good to go."

He watched patiently as she moved the lead across the paper until the imprint of Lara's handwriting was perfectly legible. "CLS," J.J. read, then presented the pad to him. "Mean anything?"

He looked at the letters, which were scribbled over and over again, followed by a phone number. He shook his head. "But then again, my cryptanalytic skills are a little rusty."

"I can call Stephenson and have—"

"I'm on it." He grabbed his cell, dialed the Marshal Service and gave them the number. "Done. Now what?"

"We need a computer. Let's Google the letters and see what happens."

"That's a high security approach," he joked.

"I'll text message my boss—at the *correct* number— and see if the cipher guys can make something of the letters."

She started toward the door but he caught her arm. "We've got a more immediate problem. You're a target and I'm running out of safe places."

"I'm a federal agent, Cody. Stop treating me like some civilian. I want your help more than I need your protection. I'm capable and I'm armed. So can you please work with me on this?"

"I've got orders, J.J."

She rolled her eyes. "So do I. Mine are to find the leak, which I can do with or without your help. Your call."

"What do you have in mind?"

"Denise can wait. She's back at the cabin at the Lucky 7, right?"

He nodded. "I'll have Seth put a deputy on her—do the occasional drive-by just to make sure she stays put." He took out his phone and made the call. "Anything else?" he asked, the cell still at his ear.

"I'll have the FBI put a tap on Lara's and Martin's phones here at the hospital. I want to know if they so much as order a pizza."

"Lara, maybe. But Martin? Why is he still on your radar?" He didn't dare risk the FBI reporting back to her that one of Martin's responsibilities was to make sure the Visnopov people had a general idea of where the marshal service was hiding their target.

Sighing, she relented. "Okay, just Lara. For now."

Once she had made her calls, and he'd finished his, Cody asked, "Any computer will do, right?"

"So long as it has Internet. DSL would be great. A wireless mouse, voice recognition."

He smiled. "A girl who likes toys, eh?"

"A *woman* who likes toys," she quipped.

It suddenly occurred to him that the J.J. Barnes who'd stepped off the plane less than ten days ago would have bitten his head off for that remark. And lectured him on the sexist nature of his comment. Quietly he regarded her for a long moment, really seeing her now that her protective shield of aggression was down.

At first, he'd only seen her physical beauty. Now he knew there was much, much more. This complex woman was stronger than most men, resilient as hell, driven and...*fun.* That was the kicker. That was what he hadn't expected. That was why he was falling in love with her.

Oh God! Could my timing be any worse?

"Are we going somewhere or what?" J.J. impatiently held the door handle, knowing full well he'd want to do his protective survey before they left the hospital.

"Yeah," he mumbled, as if her question required advanced math. "My brother's office."

"Seth?"

"Sam."

She grunted frustration as she followed him out the door. "I can't keep all these Landrys straight. It would be easier for me if we just assigned everyone a letter or a number. You know, brother A, brother B, etc. etc."

"You'll get it eventually," he promised with a chuckle. "We all have different personalities. After tomorrow's breakfast, you'll have everyone down pat."

"Not unless they wear name tags."

Cold, damp air slapped her as she stepped out of the overly warm building. Impossible as it seemed, the snow was still falling, creating huge drifts that had already swallowed many of the cars in the lot.

Two plows were operating over in the visitors' lot, trying to keep a channel open. The stench of diesel fuel spoiled the clean scent of the new snow.

"This is a real pain," she grumbled, moving as quickly as her bundled body allowed.

"You get used to it," Cody promised as he slid inside the Hummer, brushing snow from his hair. "This is just a dusting."

"How many feet does it have to snow before I can call it a storm?"

He laughed and she found the sound soothing. No, more than soothing. It was comforting. Comfortable. As if she was meant to be in *this* place with *this* man. Scary thought. It implied permanence, something she hadn't ever so much as considered. The cold must have frozen some of her brain cells. The alternative would mean she was actually feeling something for Cody. An even scarier thought.

SAM LANDRY was not just a bean counter. Not if his business was any indication. Landry and Associates occupied an entire building in the heart of Jasper. According to Cody, his brother had only recently ventured out on his own and, from the looks of it, he was doing quite well. Although the floor was dim and deserted due to the late hour, J.J. couldn't help but be struck by the art that adorned every wall from the lobby to Sam's poshly decorated office.

She went to a particular oil hanging behind the mahogany desk. It was a spectacular landscape that managed to capture a pastoral scene that looked vaguely familiar. Her eyes scanned the meadow in full bloom, rimmed by majestic mountains. The colors were perfect, real yet somehow soft and dreamy.

"C.W. Landry?" she read. "Great," she tossed over

her shoulder at Cody. "That could be you, Clayton, Chance or Chandler."

"You left out my cousin, Cade," he teased.

"The Landrys *definitely* need to think about varying the consonants."

"Of course, you'd be wrong," he said, pressing behind her and slipping his hands around her waist. "The artist is Callie Walters Landry. Sam's wife. She painted all this stuff. Sam wanted to surround himself with images of the ranch. Callie obliged."

"She's very talented, but did he really have to marry someone with a 'C' name?"

He nuzzled her neck. "Only after Seth married Savannah."

"C's and S's. I…hate…your…confusing…family," she breathlessly managed to say as her body quivered from his touch.

His hand gently massaged her belly as his hips moved against her back. "It doesn't feel like you hate me." He nibbled her earlobe.

"Not this *exact* instant. No." Cody had an incredible mouth and it was doing the most delightful things to her neck. She pressed closer, as if that was possible. A fire flared in her soul as he methodically and purposefully kissed his way across her cheek, then took her mouth. It was so good. So right.

And so over.

Her eyes flew open. She craned her neck to see Cody wearing a very satisfied smile.

"I wasn't done," she told him, vainly trying to twist in his grasp in order to continue the kiss.

"Good things come to those who wait," he promised, thwarting her efforts. "Even if the wait is becoming unbearable."

"So why make it worse?" she asked, mortified when it came out like a childish whine.

"Because, my dear Agent Barnes, the wanting is always the best part."

"That's a pretty stupid perspective," she groused as she took a seat at the computer and tried to focus on the task. Not an easy thing since he insinuated himself next to her and his nearness was a constant reminder of what she couldn't have.

"You get testy when you're frustrated, huh?"

Frustrated? Try ready to explode. "It isn't very gentlemanly to gloat."

"Probably not, but it is a lot of fun."

"You want fun? Try a board game."

She typed the letters that Lara had wanted to keep secret into a search engine. It wasn't the easiest thing in the world to do with Cody's warm breath in her ear and the heat from his large body disturbing her concentration.

She twirled in the chair and was about to give him a lecture, when her eyes connected with the painting. She had a sudden thought.

Tearing a sheet of paper from a nearby notepad, she wrote the letters in a vertical line. "C—cabin. L—Lucky. S—Seven." She glanced up at Cody. "Cabin at the Lucky 7. Our location. I think we just found the leak."

Chapter Fourteen

"So what now?"

Cody went to the window and shoved aside the drapes. While his strongest instinct was to race to the hospital and shake Lara until her teeth fell out, he needed to get his head on straight first.

"Out to the ranch."

"In this weather? And why not go back and talk to Lara? Seems to me she has some explaining to do."

"Oh, believe me, she does. And she will, just not tonight." He handed J.J. her coat.

"But if Lara did give away my location, isn't it a little dangerous to go to the ranch?"

He paused, frustration settling in the pit of his stomach. "It's as secure there as anywhere else. Seth has a unit doing drive-bys—"

"It's freezing and snowy, Cody. It's inhumane to send people out in these conditions. Surely there's another alternative."

"There's an Inn a couple miles up the road. Denise already scouted it out. We could have a hot meal, get a little sleep."

"A meal is good," she told him enthusiastically. "A meal delivered by room service is even better."

He gave her a challenging glance. "When did you turn into Pamper-Me-Princess?"

"When I missed three meals in a row and so much sleep that I couldn't possibly muster the energy to cook for myself."

"Okay, but we do this my way."

It took almost an hour and all his skills to drive the short distance to the Inn. The good news was that he doubted even a paid killer would venture out in this storm. The bad news was the Inn wasn't the secure kind of location he liked.

He pulled around to the back of the A-framed building, then down a rutted roadway.

"You did say *at* the Inn, right?"

"Just checking things out," he assured her. Swallowing a string of colorful curse words, he started to second-guess his decision. Between skiers and early arrivals for the wedding, the place was packed. Hard to secure an area when half the license plates were obscured by snow and the ones he could see included no fewer than seven different states and stickers from twice that many *counties*.

Looping back around, he cruised the parking lot again, hoping a brilliant idea would fall into his lap. None did.

"Are you going to drive around until you wear out the tires or is there an executive decision in your future?"

Pulling his cell phone out, he pressed one of the speed dial buttons and waited impatiently until the call was finally answered.

"Hello?"

"Sorry, Chandler, but I need a favor."

"When *don't* you need a favor?" came the smart-ass reply.

"How many rooms did you block at the Mountain-view Inn?"

"A dozen, why?"

"I need one."

"They're full of wedding stuff. I've got—"

"I *need* one."

"Right," Chandler said. "I'll call the front desk right now."

"Thanks, bro."

"You okay?"

"Working on it."

"Need us?"

"Hope not."

"I can have everyone there inside an hour," Chandler promised.

It wasn't an empty offer. Cody smiled, knowing full well that any or all of his brothers would walk though the storm if he asked. "I'm good, Chandler. Just need a place to crash for a while."

"You'll be here in the morning, though, right?"

"I'm planning on it."

"I hear you're bringing the leggy blond FBI agent." Chandler exaggerated his sigh into the phone.

"I hear you'd like to get married with all your teeth."

A sharp, piercing whistle came across the line. "That was very snippy, Cody."

"Snippy? When did you turn into a girl?"

"A minute *after* I thought I was going to call the desk at the Inn as a favor to you."

"You aren't a girl," Cody relented good-naturedly. Then he muttered, "Much."

"What?"

"I said I'll be in *touch*," he promised, then broke the connection.

"That Landry shorthand?" she asked.

He shrugged, tapping his fingers on the wheel as he watched the guy at the front desk. "Not really. We're men of action, not words."

"You gotta pound your chest when you say that, fella."

He grinned at her, and at the sight of the desk guy on the phone. "Thank you, Chandler."

A few minutes later, it was J.J. who was saying, "Thank you, Chandler." The *suite* was the most incredible thing she'd ever seen, with a sitting room, two large bedrooms, a powder room and her personal favorite—a master bath with every possible toiletry. It was as if someone dropped a little slice of Vienna in the middle of Montana. Not that she had ever been to Vienna, but she'd watched The Travel Channel enough to know that this was European-style luxury at its finest.

The sofa and a couple of large easy chairs in the living room were covered in rich, textured sage-green fabric. An ornate coffee table—complete with high hat and champagne glasses at the ready—and twin end tables were piled with beautifully wrapped wedding gifts, as was every flat surface.

"Can I live here forever?" she said.

"First hotel?" Cody teased, his dark eyes watching her as she went from room to room, item to item, enjoying herself immensely.

"First *first-class* hotel," she readily admitted. "This room is bigger than my apartment. And my apartment doesn't smell like—what is that?"

"These things," he said, holding out a dainty glass dish filled with potpourri as if it was a urine specimen. "Molly's idea, I'm sure. I hear she's into candles and stuff. Shane says he can always tell when Chandler's been with Molly, 'cause he comes home smelling like a florist's shop."

She blinked. Twice. "This is *their* suite?" she asked, horrified. "The bridal suite?"

"Eventually, yeah." Cody sat down, kicked off his boots and relaxed on the sofa.

"But the wedding isn't until the day after tomorrow. Why is their stuff here now?"

"Because as much as I love him—and I do—Chandler plans everything to death. He's probably got a second suite rented just in case this one…I don't know…has a leaky faucet or some other imperfection."

J.J. chewed her lip to keep from laughing. "How did he manage growing up on a ranch if he's so…particular?"

"*Because* he grew up on a ranch he's so particular," Cody corrected. "He's more organized than the National Archives. Which—" he jumped up, disappeared into a bedroom, returning a second later with a small satchel in his hand "—will work to our advantage." He rummaged through the bag and pilfered a T-shirt for J.J. to use as a nightshirt.

"I shouldn't take this," she resisted. "He might need it."

Cody grunted. "Right. What guy needs three T-shirts on his wedding night? Besides, he has all day tomorrow to replace everything so it's just the way he likes it. Red or green?" he asked, holding two brand-new, still-in-their wrapper toothbrushes up to her.

"We can use the ones the hotel provides," she said, recalling the fully stocked bath.

Cody's broad grin was infectious. "We could, but it wouldn't be as much fun."

"You can be very childish," she told him as she snatched the red one, grinning back at him.

"Only occasionally," he assured her. "And usually only when one of my brothers is involved. I figure it's the payoff for all those years of getting my tail kicked on a regular basis."

"But you're all so close."

"Now," he agreed. "Growing up was a different story. We fought like crazy when we were kids. Someone was always pounding on someone else. My mother spent a lot of her day refereeing. By the time Pop got home, we quieted down. You didn't want any part of making my father mad."

She saw fear—quick, real and palpable—flash in his eyes. "Was he harsh?"

Cody chuckled. "Harsh? Detergent is harsh. My pop was the law in our house."

"You make it sound horrible."

He shook his head, then raked his dark hair back into place. "It wasn't. I'm giving you the wrong impression. Pop was just firm. Had to be. Especially when we reached our teens. If Pop hadn't kept us in line, we'd probably all be in jail by now. He was tough, but he was always fair. Almost always," he relented. "He was roughest on Shane. I guess by the time he'd had his seventh son, he was tired of parenting period. The two of them were like oil and water, too. That didn't help the situation."

"I know what that's like."

"Really?" he asked, genuine interest in his tone. Patting the seat next to him, he said, "Sit down with me, J.J. I know a whole file of facts, but I don't really know much about you."

Reluctantly she sat down beside him. "Not much to tell. Nothing like *Life with the Landrys*."

"I bet there are a *milliner* stories you can tell me."

She elbowed him. Hard. "Again with the hat jokes?"

"Sorry, I just *cap* help myself."

"You know," she began, trying to sound affronted, which was almost impossible when he was wearing that sexy smile he probably didn't even know was sexy. "Hats don't just fall from heaven. Someone has to make them."

"And my hat's off to that person."

"Landry!" she warned, hitting him with a tasseled pillow. "Do you hear me making cow jokes? Have I mocked your family's heritage in any way?"

"No. I'm sorry, J.J., really."

"You should be. My father happens to be an honest, hardworking man."

"I'm sure he is. Must be proud of you, too."

That made J.J. laugh. "Are you crazy? He hates what

I do. Thinks it's dangerous and completely unsuitable for his only child to be off chasing bad guys."

"He's got a point there."

She swatted him again. "I'm good at what I do. I put bad people in jail. He should like what I do."

"I'm sure he'd like grandchildren more."

She'd heard that chorus before. "I bought him a dog. That should keep him for a while."

"What about your mother?" he asked, reaching out to play with her hair. He twirled a few strands gently around his index finger, then let them slip away before repeating the action.

"She got sick right before I started the Visnopov assignment."

"Is she better now?"

"She died a year ago. Cancer. My father didn't allow them to tell me while I was undercover with the Visnopovs. Said she didn't want me to know how sick she was and he didn't want me distracted after she died."

"That's rough."

"Yes, well, unlike your family, mine was not very open. It took three months for my folks to get around to telling me that my dad had lost his business. And then they only said something because we had to move."

"I'm sure they were only trying to protect you."

Suddenly feeling as if every cell in her body was made of lead, J.J. stood. "That's a justification for lying by omission," she said grimly. "Look, I'm flat-out exhausted. All I want right now is a hot bath and a solid eight hours of sleep. Night, Cody." She headed for the smaller of the bedrooms.

"J.J.?"

She turned and found his brow deeply furrowed and his mouth drawn into a taut line. "What?"

"I just want to—"

The last thing she wanted was to plan strategy or talk shop. Neither did she want to discuss the past. Walks down memory lane were exhausting. "Can we do this later?"

Cody gave her a look she couldn't interpret. He rubbed his hand across his jaw, looking as wiped out as she felt. "Sure," he told her. "Later it is."

"Night, then."

"Yeah. Night."

J.J. closed the bedroom door, trying not to wonder what he'd been about to tell her.

THE NEXT MORNING dawned quietly. In the wake of the huge, powerful storm was a vast, beautiful sky smeared with the pastel colors of a new day, and piles of soft pristine-white snow on the ground.

J.J. left the window and slipped back under the blankets, not in any great hurry to abandon the soft comfort of the best bed she'd had in days. But the aroma of coffee called to her.

Slipping on a heavy terry cloth robe with the hotel's logo embroidered on the front, she padded into the sitting room and found Cody dressed in what appeared to be a freshly laundered version of the clothing he'd worn yesterday.

Glancing around, she saw her clothing on a hanger over the closet doorknob, wrapped in plastic from the hotel cleaner.

He offered her a smile and passed her a folded sheet of paper. "Morning. This came for you."

She was about to accept his kiss on her cheek when she realized what he'd handed her. "This is a confidential fax."

"Stephenson ran down the license plate of the guy Denise was with," he said as he moved to pour her some coffee from the white carafe that dominated a large silver tray with assorted fruits and pastries on the coffee table.

She met and held his gaze. "Confidential. Cody, you do know what that word means, right?"

He didn't even try to look apologetic. "When he couldn't reach me, Stephenson sent it to Seth. Seth brought it to me. What's the harm?"

"The harm is, it's mine. Not ours. In fact, there is no *ours* when it comes to stuff like this." She rattled the page for effect. "I probably would have shared this with you, but the decision should have been mine."

"Don't get all bent out of shape. It isn't like it's the launch codes for our nuclear arsenal, J.J. If it was *really* private, I'm sure Stephenson wouldn't have sent it through Seth's office."

Crumpling the paper in her fist, she tried to control her simmering anger. "The content isn't the point, Landry. I'm explaining to you how much I resent you perusing a message addressed to me."

"I'm sorry. Want me to pretend I didn't see the name of the guy Denise met in the parking lot?"

"I want you to remember that as far as the FBI is concerned, you're a security risk. If Associate Director Andrews ever so much as suspected that I've been sharing information with you, he'd fire me in a heartbeat."

"You think he doesn't know already?" Cody challenged.

She hadn't expected the small flash of anger from him. Nor, in her opinion, was it something he was entitled to. After all, he was the one who'd read her mail, not vice versa. "I didn't tell him. Did *you?* " she shot back.

"Oh, wait." She sarcastically smacked her own forehead. "You *can't* tell him. You're not FBI. We play on different teams."

"I didn't know that," he tossed back. "I was under the impression that it didn't matter what version of the alphabet we worked for. That this was a joint effort. We may have started out differently, but I thought we've been on the same wavelength lately…am I wrong?"

She opened her mouth, then shut it abruptly.

"No," she finally said. "I am. I overreacted. I'm just not used to people being in my space. Thanks for getting my clothes cleaned."

"No problem. We won't have time to swing by the cabin before we have to be at the ranch." He shoved the coffee at her. "Can you be ready in twenty?"

"I can do it in ten."

Could she ever, he thought when she emerged from the bedroom ten minutes later. How could a woman who didn't even carry a purse manage to look so stunning in record time. If he ever figured that out, he'd sell the secret and make a mint.

"Is there a problem?" she asked, tucking her weapon into the waistband of her jeans.

"You look nice. Really nice. My brothers will be envious." He could have kicked himself for that one. He braced himself, sure she would give it to him with both barrels for making it sound like he was taking her along for show-and-tell.

Instead she surprised him by offering a sincere, almost shy smile. "Thanks to the foresight of this fabulous hotel, I found enough products to keep from looking completely scary."

"You've never been scary a day in your life." He meant it.

She cocked one brow and shook her head. "Lots of days, actually. Grades five through twelve, to be exact. I was taller than most of my teachers. I was all legs and teeth. Not a pretty sight."

Draping his arm around her shoulder, he kissed her temple and said, "It worked out, though. Quite well, if you want my opinion."

"So what's our plan?"

He grabbed their coats, then headed for the door. "First, we do the wedding thing with my family. Then it's time to kick some serious ass."

Chapter Fifteen

The roadway between Jasper and the Lucky 7 ranch was a glistening black ribbon edged by several feet of mounded snow. As improbable as it seemed, plows had already cleared what would have taken the better part of a week to handle back east.

J.J. was distracted by the blinding reflection of the sun off the vast, pristine landscape almost as much as the jumble of thoughts twisting around in her head.

Turning her whole body in the passenger seat, she studied Cody's profile for a moment. Not because she didn't have it memorized, but because he simply took her breath away. Quite an accomplishment since she wasn't exactly the swooning type. No, while she appreciated beauty as much as the next girl, it never had this kind of effect on her.

Until now.

Until her stomach fluttered just breathing in the familiar scent of him. Until her pulse raced just remembering the feel of his kiss. Until she had to admit that Cody Landry wasn't just a passing fancy. This wasn't casual interest. This wasn't lust. Nope, this was something more. Something bigger.

Love.

Saying the word in her head caused a dozen different reactions to tingle through her system. Aside from the worst possible timing in the history of male-female interaction, how could this happen? To her? With him? Now?

"Nervous about meeting my family?" he asked.

"Kinda," she lied. *Actually, Cody, I'm a tad on edge because I think I'm falling in love with you. I know this is sudden, but…but what?* her brain screamed. *Marry me?*

She gulped. The "M" word scared her almost as much as the Visnopovs did.

His palm closed over her knee and he gave a squeeze that was probably supposed to be reassuring. It wasn't. It was just another reminder that she'd seriously gone around the bend. This was the twenty-first century! They hadn't so much as gone on a date. *So how can I even think I'm falling in love with him?*

He flashed that comfortably sexy grin at her, then asked, "I could tell you embarrassing stories about my brothers if it would put you at ease."

"I'd rather get my mind off the meet-the-brothers moment. Why don't we start by you telling me why we aren't questioning Denise or Lara."

The smile slipped as his expression hardened slightly. Seeing the flicker of sadness in his chocolate eyes, J.J. experienced a pang of guilt. Sometimes it was hard to remember that these people were his friends. Betrayal was the worst.

"I'm waiting on the LUDs from Lara's hospital

phone and her cell," Cody explained. "If she is the leak, I want to make sure we have enough evidence to fry her."

Remind me not to get on his bad side. "And Denise?"

"Seth is pulling everything he can on the name Stephenson faxed over this morning. He's bringing it to the ranch. We'll go from there."

She slipped her hand over his where it rested on her knee. It looked ridiculously small and pale against the tanned breadth of his. "Wouldn't it have been easier to simply confront them?"

"I can't go off half-cocked on this, J.J. I talked to Martin this morning and he agreed. Slow and deliberate. I can't afford to get this wrong."

"How's he doing?"

She was pleased to see Cody's expression lighten. "Champing at the bit to be released from the hospital."

"Did you tell him about the notepad from Lara's room?"

He nodded. "CLS meant nothing to him right off the bat, but he's going to work on it."

"As soon as we get to the ranch, I'll call Stephenson and see if I can't light a fire under him," J.J. promised.

One dark eyebrow arched in her direction. "Is that so you'll have an excuse not to participate in the final wedding strategy session?"

She offered a guilty smile. "Of course. Besides, I'd only be in the way. You make sure to have fun, though."

"You can be cruel, Agent Barnes."

"So I've been told."

IT SHOULD BE illegal to have so many Landrys in one place. They were loud, boisterous and in serious need of a professional wedding planner. From her seat in the roomy kitchen, J.J. could hear lively debates over everything from the seating chart for the reception to whether it was too late to change the nail polish requirements for the bridal attendants.

So how come *I'm envious?* J.J. wondered as she dialed the Helena field office and asked to be put through to Stephenson.

"Stephenson."

"Barnes here," J.J. said, using her most professional tone. "You sent a fax to the town sheriff?"

"Only because I didn't know your location," Stephenson returned quickly. "You never checked in, Barnes. I forwarded that to your superiors in Washington."

Weasel. "What do you have for me?" *Besides guaranteeing a Letter of Reprimand.*

"Who do you want first?"

"Cod—Landry," she said, glad she caught herself in time.

J.J. got up to help herself to coffee as she listened to Stephenson shuffle papers, then begin to speak. "He was careful, but I managed to trace several bank withdrawals over the last few months. All cash, and I can't account for any of it."

I can, you ferret. He was using the money to pay a P.I. to hunt for his folks. "Keep digging," she instructed, enjoying the fantasy of Stephenson hunched over a computer, hunting for something he'd never trace.

Cody was too smart for that. Stephenson, apparently, was not.

"Since you're in Montana, we sent field agents in California, Seattle and Miami to do interviews on Howard, Newell and Selznick."

J.J. groaned. "They aren't supposed to know we're investigating them."

"They don't," Stephenson insisted. "Just because I'm not from the D.C. or New York office doesn't mean I'm incompetent, Barnes. The field agents are conducting interviews with friends and family under the guise of routine security background checks. You gotta love The Patriot Act."

"Anything turn up?" She sipped her coffee, then sat down again at the large oak table to listen to the report.

"Denise Howard's husband, Greg, was really, really nervous, according to the report. He answered all the questions put to him, but the field agent noted he was sweating bullets the whole time and it had nothing to do with the sunny California weather. They're canvassing the neighborhood today to see if anything turns up.

"The agent who went to the Newells' apartment in Seattle bombed out. Mrs. Newell wasn't home and she wasn't at work. Co-worker said she had a doctor's appointment this morning, so they're going back this afternoon."

"Is she sick?"

"Maybe," Stephenson supplied. "One of her co-workers let it slip that Mrs. Newell has been having some female problems. She's in her forties. Isn't that about the time you ladies start to break down?"

"It's called premenopause, you moron." An idea

made it through the fog of her irritation. "Does she have health insurance?"

More shuffling of papers. "Yep. Employer-provided HMO. Secondary to being covered on her husband's plan."

So much for that theory. "What about Lara Selznick?"

"Now here's an interesting little tidbit I bet you don't know about Lara Selznick."

J.J. resisted rolling her eyes. "And what might that be?"

"Lara Selznick doesn't exist."

"DON'T YOU FIND that strange?" she asked him for the third time since they'd left the ranch.

"None of her neighbors knows anything about her?" He rubbed his chin, still digesting all the information J.J. had shared.

"None. Zero. Zippo. A twenty-unit apartment complex and not one person has ever interacted with Lara other than to say 'hello' in the elevator or the laundry room. And," she continued on a rush of breath, "it's one of those Florida snowbird buildings. Lara is the only tenant who lives there year-round. And she's like *three* generations younger than everyone else in the place."

"She's on the road a lot," Cody qualified. "There could be a dozen reasons why she lives there."

"Name one," J.J. challenged as he turned onto the highway and headed toward the cabin.

"Cheap rent."

"Okay. Name another."

"No kids."

He watched her deflate out of the corner of his eyes.

"Or, she could be using the place as a front to plan the overthrow of the government. My point is, all we have are some letters and a phone number on a pad and a description of her living arrangements that sounds pretty dull."

"But no one *knows* her," J.J. argued.

Glancing over at her, he asked, "Where do you live?"

"I have an apartment in Arlington, Virginia. Why?"

"Who are your neighbors?"

"I—I haven't been there much for two years."

"Before that? Before you went undercover. Did you throw dinner parties? Get together for a wild canasta night?"

"No. But I'm not seventy and I don't know how to play canasta. What's your point?"

"That you aren't so different from Lara." He heard an indignant little snort from her direction and fought back a smile.

"What about you?" she challenged.

Cody's urge to smile vanished. "Guilty. I have an apartment in D.C that I've slept in *maybe* fifty nights in five years. But—" he felt a surge of arrogance "—I do know that my next-door neighbor likes to watch court shows and yell at the litigants. That's something."

"Yeah," J.J. fairly jeered. "It's lame. We are a sad group, Cody, aren't we?"

"We have demanding jobs that don't lend themselves to having lives," he said as the cabin came into sight.

"I used to think that was a good thing," she mused.

Me, too, he thought as the tire caught a patch of slick snow, careening him into the driveway. He just missed smashing into the side of the SUV.

Just as he reached for the door handle, J.J. reached for him. There was quiet concern in her eyes.

"I know this is tough on you."

He managed a weak smile. "Interrogating Denise probably won't be the best part of my day."

"Want me to wait here?"

He shook his head. "You can't wait out here. You're still a target, remember?"

She reached up and placed her palm against his cheek. "You're wearing too many hats on this one. Landry. Why not let me interrogate Denise and you stay out here. After all, this is my investigation."

"And you are the expert on hats."

J.J. smiled in spite of herself. "I'm *so* sorry I told you about my milliner skills. Had I known you were going to work in a hat pun at every turn, I'd never have said a word."

She felt his return grin through all three layers of clothing. When he lifted his hand to cup her face, she watched—fascinated—as his gaze turned to luscious liquid chocolate. His attention was squarely fixed on her mouth and she could almost feel the kiss before it actually happened.

He surprised her, though. This kiss was different. Tentative, curious, sweet. The passion was there—as always, but this time he slowly and deliberately took her mouth with a gentleness that she hadn't expected.

It triggered in her something primal and needy. Her whole body felt coiled. There was nothing tentative in the way she yanked at the zipper of his jacket and shoved her hands inside to feel the corded strength of his torso.

She deepened the kiss, changing the tenor to convey her total and complete need for this man. She reveled in the warm wetness of his mouth, sparred with his tongue, nibbled his lips. But it wasn't enough. Not nearly enough.

His hands moved to her shoulders, firmly grasping her in order to basically pry her off of him. She should have been embarrassed. But she wasn't. She was just too needy.

He looked at her with heavy, hooded eyes, his breaths coming in short, shallow gulps. "We're fogging up the windows."

J.J. glanced around. "So we are."

"Denise is going to march out here—" He stopped in midsentence.

Instantly, J.J. realized the ramifications of the situation as her training superceded her longings. "Why *didn't* she march out here?" She wasn't sure why she was whispering as she reached for her weapon in concert with Cody.

Grabbing his phone, he called Denise. J.J. lowered the window a crack and could hear the faint chime of the cell phone ringing inside the cabin. No answer.

After dialing 9-1-1, he said, "Stay behind me."

"I'll check the SUV."

Cody shot her a stern look and pointed to himself. "U.S. Marshal." He pointed at her. "Protectee." Next, he opened the door and practically dragged her across the console, shielding her as she stumbled out of the car.

Guns drawn, they flattened against the cold steel of the SUV and worked their way around to the back of the vehicle with the effortless precision of synchronized swimmers. Knowing the cars were their best barricade should anyone be inside the cabin, J.J. worked as a team with Cody. He opened a door, she dropped on one knee, gun targeting the area.

After they'd checked the SUV, J.J. followed Cody as they used the dash and cover method to work their way to the porch.

Careful to avoid the windows, J.J. felt her heart pounding from the rush of adrenaline as she watched Cody mouth a count of three before he reared back and kicked in the door.

It hit her instantly.

The acrid, sour smell of death.

Chapter Sixteen

"This says Visnopov all over it," J.J. told Seth as the medical examiner zipped the body bag.

Seth nodded, pushing the Stetson back on his head. "Classic execution, I'd say. Back of the head. Close range. A .22 by the looks of it."

Cody stormed over, his face pinched with fury as he began barking orders. "I want every inch of this place dusted for prints. Have the state CSIs on their hands and knees with tweezers and tape. I want every fiber, skin cell and blood drop bagged, tagged and processed. Yesterday."

J.J. was about to say something when Seth took Cody by the arm and practically shoved him from the room. She heard Seth launch into a litany of promises in a brotherly tone that she only hoped could salve some of Cody's emotions.

Taking a pair of latex gloves from one of the crime scene techs, J.J. snapped them on and began to look around. Her stomach lurched at the sights. Remnants of Visnopov brutality were everywhere. Guilt formed a choking lump in her throat. Intellectually, she knew this was not her fault. But knowing something on an intellectual level and feeling it squeeze your emotions were completely unrelated things. Denise may have known the risks—accepted them even—but that didn't make her brutal murder any easier to handle.

"Was this photographed?" she called over her shoulder. She crouched down alongside the overturned dinette.

"Yes, ma'am."

She slipped a manila envelope from under shards of broken glass, careful to avoid the blood splatters. She guessed it was the same envelope Denise had gotten from the mystery man the day before. If it had something to do with the Visnopovs, they wouldn't have left it behind.

J.J. pushed up the silver tabs, fed them through the little metal hole, and opened the envelope.

The top sheet was a cover letter from Huntley Tarrelton, III, Esq. J.J. snorted. A name like that pretty much destined a guy to be an attorney. She was about to begin reading the rest of the contents when a more collected Cody appeared at her side.

"Find something?"

She stood, hearing her knee crack in the process. "Maybe. Tax returns."

Cody read over her shoulder as she skimmed through five years of joint returns signed by Denise and her husband, Greg. When she finished, she glanced up at Cody, trying to decide if he'd managed to make any sense out of the endless, neatly typed schedules and forms.

"Maybe the forensic accountants can do something with this stuff," she suggested.

Cody took the stack. "I'm going to give Sam a crack first. It'll be faster."

She was about to remind him that doing so violated chain of evidence and would probably render any information inadmissible, but one look at the determined set of his jaw convinced her otherwise. "Okay."

"I called my boss, as well as Martin and Lara."

"How did they take it?"

He shrugged. "About how you'd expect. The Marshal Service is pulling together another detail. They should—"

"No!" J.J. practically yelled. "I mean—Cody?"

He hurried her from the crime scene, barely giving her time to remove her latex gloves or put on her coat. "What are you doing?" she demanded, almost out of breath by the time he'd rushed her into the car.

"I'm driving you to Helena. Four new marshals are arriving on the five o'clock flight. They'll pick you up and take you to a new location."

"I don't want four new marshals," she insisted, folding her arms in front of her. "I don't want *any* marshals, period. I just got one killed. I don't want any more deaths on my head."

She watched as his fingers tightened on the steering wheel. He stared straight ahead, a vein twitching at his temple.

"This is not negotiable," he insisted through clenched teeth.

"We agree on that," she returned, matching his tone.

"I can't protect you here, J.J. But I'll damned sight make sure you're someplace where the Visnopovs can't find you until I sort this out."

She glared at him as anger churned in her stomach.

"I don't need you to protect me. I need to find the leak and I'm pretty sure it's Lara."

"So am I," he agreed.

The subtle fury in his tone gave her pause. "Which means you need to take yourself out of the loop."

He snorted angrily at her. "Not going to happen. Martin and I have already worked this out with the full support of my superiors."

"Good for you. Good for Martin. Good for your superiors. But you seem to have forgotten something, Landry. Finding the leak is *my* assignment. I'm seeing this through to the end." She paused to take a quick breath. "My boss trusted me with this assignment. I am—"

"Your boss hung you in the breeze!" Cody exploded, whipping his head around in time to see the shock register on her face. Too late. He couldn't take it back. "That's right, Agent Barnes. Your boss came up with this whole charade. My team and I were *supposed* to let the Visnopovs get close enough to take a crack at you."

She went very still and he could almost hear the wheels in her brain turn. It seemed like forever before she said, "Get the killers. Flip the killers to find the leak. Flip the leak and get hard evidence against Visnopov on the three witness murders."

"Right."

"Wrong." She turned, looking at him with an expression that made him evaporate. "It could have been four murders. I was expendable in this operation, right?"

"J.J.—" Her name came out like a plea as he reached for her.

She stiffened against the car door, holding up a single finger in a warning. "Do not touch me right now."

"Hey." He put up both hands. "Don't shoot the messenger. I didn't like it when I was given the assignment, and I like it even less now."

"That's a different discussion. Right now, we're going to focus on making this work."

"Making what work?" he asked.

"As much as it ticks me off that I wasn't brought into the loop at the onset, I'm a professional, for God's sake. Face it. It's a solid plan."

Rage, fierce and primal, coursed through every cell in his body. "Are you nuts?" He ignored the fact that, even though they were inside the Hummer with the windows up and the doors locked, every technician and officer around the cabin was staring in their direction. "There isn't a hope in this big world that I'll sit back and let you take that kind of risk."

"I'm sorry," she snapped sarcastically. "Was there a question mark after that statement? Nope. I wasn't asking for your permission, Landry. I don't need it."

"You sure as hell do!" he shouted.

"Why?" J.J. shouted back.

"Because I'm in love with you."

She blinked twice. Then reared back and slapped him. Hard.

"ARE WE going to talk about it?" he asked later that morning.

"No," she said, not turning away from the task of

clipping tags from her new clothes before placing them neatly on hangers.

Cody dominated the doorway that separated her bedroom from the living room of the three-room bungalow. Though it was part of the Mountainview Inn where they'd stayed the night before, it wasn't quite as posh as the honeymoon suite. Still, it was nice. And it was moderately accessible. Practically an invitation for the Visnopovs to make another attempt on her life.

She wouldn't even look at him. In truth, she couldn't. Not when her brain was replaying "Because I'm in love with you!" over and over in the most annoying mantra.

One of the Landrys—a "C" wife or an "S" wife, or maybe Taylor—had kindly gone shopping at the local store and sent over an elaborate replacement wardrobe to keep J.J. from having to wear the same jeans and sweater for the remainder of her time in Jasper. Whoever it was did a nice job. Save for one thing. The dress.

Not just any dress. A stunning aqua gown, handbeaded and sixty dollars more expensive than the sticker price on her first car. J.J. wasn't cutting the tags off that. It was going back. As were the perfect shoes, the chandelier earrings and matching cuff bracelet. All going back.

"Why did she buy this?" she muttered, trying to convince herself that it would be wrong to even consider trying it on.

"The wedding is formal," Cody supplied.

"And full of people," she reminded him. "Not that I'd go anyway."

"I'm going, so you're going."

"I'll stay here. Martin can pretend to guard me. Or Lara. It doesn't really matter, does it? I mean—" she paused and looked at his unyielding expression "—the point is to give the mob an opening to make their move. Not having you here might inspire them to go for it. They get caught before, during or after and then—"

It took only three steps for Cody to reach her, grab her upper arms and say, "Don't say that, J.J. I know you're pissed at me and feeling flippant."

She lifted her eyes but not her chin, intentionally. She batted her lashes and donned a particularly chilly smile. "Now why would I be pissed, Landry? Oh, yeah. You were using me as bait and didn't bother to mention it. Pretty unreasonable and petty of me to be pissed about that."

His grasp loosened. "Not unreasonable," he relented. "And not the whole truth, either. I think you're mad because I told you how I feel about you. Because I had enough guts to be honest."

"When it suited you," she calmly reminded him. "As far as I know, the whole 'I love you' thing could have been a ploy to get me to go to Helena to be handed off to the backup team. You've been lying to me from minute one, so don't you dare be surprised if I don't have much faith in what comes out of your mouth right now."

He sighed heavily. "Fair enough. Martin and Lara will be here any minute. How do you want to play it?"

"I don't want Lara to know I suspect her just yet,"

J.J. said in her most efficient, professional tone. "Can you get Martin out of here for a little while?"

"Why?"

"Because I'm handling this my way." She gave him a look that fairly dared him to argue, then said, "Deal with it."

"I can send him back to Helena. The forensic reports got misplaced when they towed the sedan in after the accident. Either someone at the garage has a morbid sense of curiosity or the crime scene techs collected them not realizing they were copies of their own evidence. Either way, we'll need the reports."

LARA ARRIVED about a half hour later, still wearing a sling and a very sour expression. Martin stayed only long enough to get his instructions before Cody tossed him the keys to the Hummer, then heard him drive off.

After surveying the three-room bungalow, Lara seemed to relax. She moved into the kitchenette and opened the refrigerator, leaning in to pull a bottle of water from the top shelf.

Cody and J.J. were seated at the small, round table in the living room. Using the tip of his boot, Cody pushed out the chair across the table from him and said, "Take a load off."

Lara's pale brown eyes darted back and forth. Cody knew that look. He'd seen it enough times before. Lara wore her suspicion like a badge.

"What's up?" she asked, sitting, but not comfortably. Taking a pen from his pocket, Cody wrote the letters and the telephone number on a napkin and slid it across the table toward Lara.

"Is this a test?" she asked, revealing absolutely nothing.

"You tell us, you wrote them," J.J. said.

Lara shoved the napkin back in Cody's direction, suggesting he do something physically impossible in the process. She then turned her anger on J.J. "I got blown up because of you, Barnes. If you think I'm going to sit here and listen while the two of you make accusations, you're crazy."

Lara turned back to Cody. "I've never given you a single reason to question me, my motives or my integrity," she said, slamming the untouched bottle of water on the table. "If you have proof that I've done anything to jeopardize her or the other witnesses, turn me over to the authorities. Until then, the both of you can rot in hell. I need some air."

Grabbing the keys to the SUV from the center of the table, Lara stormed out on a burst of anger and a blast of cold air, closing the door hard enough to make the picture frames rattle against the walls.

"That went well," Cody remarked as he raked his fingers through his hair.

"Actually," J.J. began, her expression utterly serious, "it did."

"How do you figure?"

"I arranged for Stephenson to put a tail on Lara."

He felt his brow furrow. "Because you're psychic and you knew she'd leave?"

J.J. shrugged. "It's what I would have done in a similar situation."

"Really?"

She nodded and leaned her elbows on the table. "Sure. That's why I wouldn't let you tell Martin our location until he was on his way here. And why I made sure you gave him explicit instructions *not* to tell Lara our new location. She had no idea until they walked through the door that we rented this place. If she is the leak, she needs to get in contact with the Visnopovs to let them know where we are. Or…"

"Or what?" Cody prompted.

J.J. gave him a devilish grin. "Or she's justifiably furious because she hasn't done anything wrong, in which case, she's furious with you and needs time to get her temper in check."

"What if there isn't a leak?" Cody suggested. "What if the Visnopovs are just *that* good."

"To have tracked and killed three witnesses while in protective custody?" J.J. asked. "And Denise? It doesn't seem likely."

Cody's cell phone chimed and he brought it to his ear. "Landry."

"Landry."

He felt himself smile. "Hi, Sam. What are you up to?"

"Shirking all wedding duties—thanks for that, by the way."

"No problem," Cody said.

"I've reviewed the tax returns. Seth should be dropping them by any minute."

"Anything interesting?"

"*Lots* of anythings," Sam answered. "I wrote you a memo. It's with the papers. I've got Roger waiting for me at the bank. Call me in about an hour if you have questions."

"Thanks, Sam."

As he hung up the phone, he saw J.J. hiding a yawn behind her hand. "Why don't you go grab a nap."

"Because I'm not two?"

"Neither one of us have had a decent night's sleep in forever."

"What are you going to do?"

He told her about Seth's impending arrival, then ushered her into the bedroom. He lingered long enough to catch sight of her lying on the bed with her hair splayed against the pillow. After she closed her eyes, he allowed himself a moment to fantasize.

She smiled at him. The expression reaching all the way into the stunning aqua depths of her eyes.

He went to the bed and pulled her into the circle of his arms. J.J. closed her eyes and placed her cheek against his chest.

Her fingers danced over his spine, leaving a trail of electrifying sensation in their wake. Passion surged inside him. She ignited feelings so powerful and so intense, he knew with absolute certainty he was in love.

He moved his hand to her rib cage, just under the swell of her breast. He wanted—no, needed— to see her face. He wanted to see the desire in her eyes. Catching her chin between his thumb and forefinger, he tilted her head up with the intention of searching her eyes. He never made it that far.

His gaze was riveted to her lips, which were slightly parted, a glistening shade of pale rose. His eyes roamed over every delicate feature and he could feel her heart rate increase through the thin fabric of her nightgown. A knot formed in his throat as he silently acknowledged his incredible need for this woman.

Lowering his head, he took that first, tentative taste. Her mouth was warm and pliant, so was her body, which now pressed urgently against him. His hands roamed purposefully, memorizing every nuance and curve.

He felt his own body respond with an ache, then an almost overwhelming rush of desire as her arms slid around his waist, pulling him closer. He marveled at the perfect way they fit together. It was as if J.J. had been made for him. For this.

He toyed with a lock of her hair, then slowly wound his hand through the silken mass and gave a gentle tug, forcing her head back even more. Looking down at her face, he knew there was no other sight on earth as beautiful and inviting as her sultry, aqua eyes.

With a single finger, he traced the delicate outline of her mouth. Her skin was the color of ivory, with a faint rosy flush.

Lowering her onto her back, he began showering her face and neck with light kisses. While his mouth searched for that sensitive spot at the base of her throat, he felt her fingers working the buttons of his shirt.

He waited breathlessly for the feel of her hands on his body. A pleasurable moan spilled from his mouth when she brushed away his clothing and began running her palms over the tensed muscles of his stomach.

Capturing both of her hands in one of his, he gently held them above her head. The position arched her back, drawing his eyes down to her erect nipples. He slowly began peeling away her silk nightgown.

J.J. responded by lifting her body to him. The rounded swell of one exposed breast brushed his arm. He stopped peeling and gave a quick and effective tug. He was rewarded by the incredible sight of her breasts spilling over a lacy undergarment. His eyes burned as he drank in the sight of the taut peaks straining against the lace. His hand rested against the flatness of her stomach before inching up over the warm flesh, his fingers closing over the rounded fullness. His thumb and forefinger released the front clasp on her bra. He ignored her futile struggle to release her hands as he dipped his head to kiss the raging pulse point at her throat. Her soft skin grew hot as he worked his mouth lower and lower. She gasped when his mouth closed around her nipple, then called his name in a hoarse voice that caused a tremor to run the full length of his body.

He lifted his head only long enough to see her passion-laden expression and to tell her she was beautiful.

He reached down until his fingers made contact with a wisp of silk and lace. The feel of the sensuous garment against her skin very nearly pushed him over the edge. With her help, he was able to whisk the panties over her hips and legs, until she was finally under him without a single barrier.

He sought her mouth again as he released his hold on her hands. He didn't know which was more potent, the feel of her naked body against his, or the frantic way she worked to remove his clothing. His body moved to cover hers again, and his tongue thrust deeply into the warm recesses of her mouth. His hand moved downward, skimming the side of her body all the way to her thigh. Then, giving in to the urgent need pulsating through him, he positioned himself between her legs. Every muscle in his body tensed as he looked at her face before directing his attention lower to the point where they would join. And then...

Seth came.

Chapter Seventeen

"You okay?" Seth slapped the manila folder into Cody's stomach. "You're sweating."

"I've been hot for a while," Cody muttered.

Seth regarded him for a long moment, looked into the bedroom, then started laughing.

Irritated at his brother, at his own transparency, at the world in general, Cody growled, "Shut up. J.J. is sleeping."

"Do I want to know what you were doing?" Seth joked. "And aren't you a little old to be doing it?"

"I would like to hurt you," Cody shot back, smacking Seth's Stetson off with the envelope. "Have a minute to sit down? I need someone to talk to."

Seth's brows arched and he donned a completely annoying smirk. "Tell me everything," he insisted, turning a chair around before taking a seat, arms folded, chin resting on his hands. "As your older brother, it's my job and my personal honor to be available to you in what is so obviously your hour of need. Hour may be a stretch. Five, ten minutes top. But go ahead, tell me everything. Well…not everything. Only the parts that include blond, leggy, *naked* FBI agents of the female persuasion."

"I only pretended to like you when we were growing up," Cody shared, taking a seat. "I don't think I will talk to you, after all."

Seth's demeanor changed to something a little more appropriate. "What's up?"

"I blew it, bro. I said something in the heat of the moment and now I can't take it back."

Seth let out a low whistle. "Not good. A woman's mind is like wet cement. Whatever you say gets imprinted on it and it's there forever. Never, I mean *never* say anything to a woman you don't want repeated back to you—*verbatim*—ten years down the road."

Cody felt himself scowl. "That's the problem. I do want it repeated back to me."

Seth's eyes opened wider and a slow, aggravating grin curled his lips. "You're in love with her." Then his expression quickly changed to concern. "Or, you said you were in love with her and you aren't?"

"I am," Cody insisted. "Which is loony in and of itself because we haven't even had a damned date, let alone sle—*just let it alone.*"

He watched as Seth relaxed back into tempered amusement. "So, your job was to try and get the girl killed, but instead, you fall in love with her. Do I have the gist of it?"

Cody cringed. That sounded really pathetic. "I have an idea. Why don't you raise your hand when you have something constructive to offer?"

Seth leaned over and patted his shoulder. "Cody, just accept that you screwed up and fix it."

"How?"

He shrugged and got to his feet. "Apologies usually go a long way. Start there."

"She won't even discuss it with me," Cody admitted.

"Maybe because she's got a few other things on her plate?" Seth suggested. "Let this whole Russian mob thing play out, then go from there. Speaking of going—" Seth pulled keys from his pocket "—I've got your tux in my jeep. Chandler packed you a bag—he must have been a girl in a past life."

"We're the same size," Cody reminded his brother, though he did chuckle at the thought. "Thank him for me."

"Thank him yourself. He and Molly should be at the Inn later. Doing something important, no doubt. Like running lint brushes over all six hundred napkins."

"That was harsh." Cody tried to take the high road and keep from grinning, but it wasn't possible. He knew full well Seth's assessment probably wasn't far off the mark.

"THIS WAS A WASTE of time," J.J. complained in a garbled version of English to Chance, whom she now thought of as Brother B, since he was the second Landry she'd met.

"Better to be safe than sorry," he insisted. "And no talking with the thermometer in your mouth."

J.J. was in bed, disheveled and a little groggy since she hadn't expected a house call from the doctor. Apparently it was her punishment for not making a follow-up appointment as directed. Cody had just shaken her awake and announced that Brother B was here.

"Your pulse is good and you have no temperature. I'd say you're good to go."

"I could have told you that," J.J. replied. "Not that I have anyplace to go."

"The wedding," Chance announced, as if it was a foregone conclusion.

She looked him directly in the eye. "I don't think that's smart or safe."

Chance gave a dismissive wave with one hand. "We've got you covered, J.J. We hired security—we've used them before—so no one will be able to get within a mile of the wedding or the reception."

She shook her head. "I'm not going to risk it."

"Cody!"

The bedroom door opened and Cody rushed in, his face tight with concern. "Is everything okay?"

"Healthwise, yes. But I'm pretty sure you wasted your money on that dress. Says she isn't going."

Cody had bought that dress? That incredible, sinfully expensive, beautiful dress?

"Thanks for dropping by," Cody told his brother. Then he pretty much shoved him to the front door. "See you tonight at dinner!" And with that, Chance was history.

J.J. used the time to put on her sweater and comb her fingers through her hair. She was one step out of the bedroom when she nearly collided with Cody. He looked determined. He looked resolute.

He looked hot.

Oh great! How was she ever going to carry on what promised to be a spirited debate when every one of her hormones was tingling with delight. He'd changed into a pair of navy slacks and a gunmetal gray shirt. Only the top two buttons were undone, giving her just a peek at the mat of dark hair she already knew covered the broad expanse of his muscular chest. How was she supposed to stay focused when he looked so...*perfect?*

"Let's discuss this rationally," he began, taking her hand and urging her to the small sofa. "I can't be in two places at once."

His cologne was wonderful...kind of woodsy.

"We've hired a private security firm."

His leg was warm where it brushed hers.

"Believe me, J.J., I wouldn't put anyone in dang—"

"I really want you."

He jerked slightly, which was pretty much the only reason she realized she had spoken aloud. Her admission hung in the space between them.

Her heart squeezed when she finally put enough brain cells together to realize that for whatever reason, he had not taken her confession as a compliment. In fact, judging by the set of his jaw and the clench of his teeth, he wasn't too pleased with her accidental honesty. "I don't know why you look so...so *affronted.* I'd think you'd like to know that I feel a certain physical attraction to you."

"Then you would be wrong," he said, his tone as distant as she'd ever heard it. "Martin's on his way back from Helena and I left a message for Lara to show up before dinner, so, I'd like to finish this conversation while we're still alone."

"Which conversation?" she retorted. "My *unwanted* physical attraction to you or the idiotic notion that I'm going to the wedding with you?"

His eyes narrowed. "The adult one. The one regarding the wedding."

She held out her hands and ticked things off on her fingers as she spoke. "Very public location. Two locations actually, church and reception. Throngs of people—including children. No time to do background checks on staff and servers. No time to do background checks on friends and guests. And—" she faltered slightly "—I can't wear that dress."

He blew a breath toward the ceiling. "The security company is at the church as we speak. Complete with bomb-sniffing dogs. Once they've done a sweep, they'll post someone until after the ceremony. They're bringing the dogs here to the Inn when they finish at the church.

"Any guest currently registered here who isn't an invitee to the wedding is being relocated by private charter to Estes Park in Colorado. They're all thrilled, by the way. Molly and Chandler provided the guests' names and the hotel turned over the employee names to the Marshal Service and the security company, so background checks will be completed by midnight tonight."

"How did you do all this?"

He shrugged. "What fun is having money if you don't spend some every now and again."

"Not out of your own pocket!" she cried. "We're federal employees, Cody. We have rules and—"

"I'm not missing this wedding, J.J.," he practically yelled at her. "I failed my family by not being able to find my parents in time to get them here. I failed in my assignment because I lost a deputy. And I pretty much screwed up where you're concerned. So, stop arguing with me. You *will* put on that damned dress and go to the wedding. Got it?"

"Uh…sure." She wanted to make a smart remark, but thought better of it. He was pretty mad and she figured it was probably best to leave it alone. For now.

Sighing, Cody pressed his fingers to his temples. "Would you please call Stephenson and ask him where Lara is?"

"No problem." J.J. went into the bedroom, retrieved her cell and placed the call. Stephenson answered on the second ring. "It's me," she said into the mouthpiece. "Where are you?"

"Sitting in a surveillance van, freezing my butt off in the parking lot of a convenience store north of you."

"Because?"

"Our girl has been on a pay phone for the better part of two hours."

"Did you get a trace?"

"About ten minutes ago. It's the same number she called like twenty-five times from her hospital room…3-0-5 area code."

"Miami." J.J. hunted around for a pen and paper, found them and said, "Give it to me." He called out the numbers. J.J. repeated them back as she wrote them down. "Reverse directory?"

"Having it faxed to you at the Mountainview Inn."

"That's convenient," she groaned.

"There aren't that many of us in the Helena office," he whined. "I'm a field agent, Barnes, not your personal assistant. What'd you expect me to do? I'm stuck out here until she decides to get off the frigging phone. Or, I can go to the office, pick up the reverse directory and bring it to your nice, warm location."

"Stay on Lara. I'll get the fax." She glanced over at Cody, lowered her voice and asked, "What about the other things? The number?"

"There is no listing in any state for the number you gave. But I'm working on it."

"Good." She hung up without thanking the guy. Jeez! You'd think he was the only agent ever stuck in a surveillance van. She'd done it more times than she could count. It came with the job.

She rejoined Cody in the living room and shared the gist of her conversation. Well, most of it anyway.

Grabbing the phone off the end table, he rang the front desk and asked if Chandler and Molly had arrived. After a pause, he directed any incoming fax for J.J. be given to his brother, Chandler.

"I can get my own mail," J.J. protested. She had to be careful. If she protested too strenuously, he'd know she was up to something.

"Barring something along the lines of a nuclear explosion, you're not leaving this bungalow until the wedding."

Okay. Problem, but not insurmountable. She'd have to text message Stephenson as soon as possible and make sure he understood the minor change in plans.

"Seth dropped these off," he told her, dropping the folder in her lap. "I'll save you some mind-numbing reading. Denise and her husband were cheating on their taxes."

"A lot?" she murmured as she scanned the memo.

"Al Capone style cheating. Sam ran the numbers and estimated they'd do at least ten years, if not more. No wonder she'd been so distracted. He also checked with an IRS contact of his. Four months ago, Denise and her husband were notified that they'd be audited."

She glanced up in response to the haunted quality of his voice. "You couldn't have guessed that, Cody."

"I might have been able to help if she'd only have asked."

"Hey, Super Deputy," she teased, tugging on the sleeve of his crisp shirt, "people who cheat the government eventually get caught. Denise knew that when she made the decision to help her husband hide income offshore."

"Money makes people do strange things," he offered, pacing nervously.

"Lack of money."

"Excuse me?"

J.J. shrugged. "It's the lack of money, Cody. An awful lot of criminals are motivated by greed for money. Denise and her husband are no different. They gave into temptation. It happens."

"Maybe the Visnopovs found out about their tax fraud," he suggested, stroking the faint stubble on his chin. "I hate to have Greg arrested on the same day he's notified of Denise's death, but it might be unavoidable."

"If she was in their pocket, they wouldn't have killed her, Cody. At least not until after they knew I was dead."

"Unless they were sending a warning to her husband," he suggested. "Maybe killing Denise was a—"

"Doesn't play," she cut in. "If Denise was the leak, they needed her alive to help them. Now, if they had killed her husband, I'd be the first one to say it was a message sent to keep her in line."

"You're right."

He rolled his head around on his shoulders. She could see the tension etched around his eyes and mouth and felt incredible empathy for him. Okay, empathy wasn't all she felt. But it was all she was willing to acknowledge. For now.

"So, we're left with Lara and the mysterious phone calls," she said. "Is your brother going to bring the fax over anytime soon?"

Cody flipped open his cell. "I'll see what's holding him up."

She heard one half of a very brief conversation, then Cody put the phone back in his pocket. "He'll take a break and run it down."

"Good. You know, we've kind of dismissed—"

Martin burst in the door then, his arms laden with a thick brown accordion file, his cheeks red.

"Didn't hear you drive up," Cody said.

"Parked up the hill. I couldn't get past the van blocking the access road. I hope we can order food before we have to start reading forensics," Martin began. "The sight of that caterer's truck made my mouth water. I haven't eaten since the hospital. And you know what they say about hospital food, so…"

J.J.'s mind went into overdrive as Martin's words turned into an undecipherable monotone of, "Blah, blah, blah."

"Is there an event tonight?" she demanded, grabbing Cody by the arm.

"No."

Without thinking, she dashed from the room with Cody fast on her heels. "J.J., wait! What are you doing?"

She raced toward the white truck parked at the top

of the hill, glancing back to see Cody gaining on her and Martin farther back.

Pulling her gun from the waistband of her jeans, J.J. approached the panel truck slowly, eyes darting around, alert for any potential danger.

"FBI! Step out of the truck!" she called.

Nothing.

Cody was now beside her, weapon drawn. She tilted her head, indicating he should approach the van from the opposite side. J.J. focused on the driver's door.

Nothing.

Her shoulder brushed the van, catching the corner of the magnetic sign in the weave of her sweater. Fancy Foods Catering peeled away to reveal Hank's Truck Rental painted in bright orange lettering.

"Truck's bogus!" she warned.

"Truck's clear," Cody called back.

"Truck's empty," Martin announced at the same time.

"Truck's rented!" called a rather frightened-looking man J.J. put someplace in his early twenties. "Who are you guys?" he asked from the safety of his hiding place in the bushes.

"Agent Barnes. FBI. Step out where we can see you, sir."

The man's blue eyes turned into wide saucers as he sidestepped his way out from behind the hedges, spindly arms raised. "I didn't do anything wrong, Miss Officer, ma'am."

"Where's your license, son?" Cody asked, stuffing his gun into his waistband as he walked over to the scared guy.

"Back right pocket."

J.J. lowered her weapon but not her guard until she saw Cody pull a tattered nylon wallet out and verify the driver's license photo before showing it to her.

"So, tell me, William—or do you prefer Bill?"

"W-Willy," the young man replied, gulping.

"Okay, Willy, what's with the van?"

"I got hired to drive it out here is all."

"By whom?" J.J. asked.

Willy's teeth began to chatter. "A-a lady c-came in and r-rented it. S-she had the signs r-ready to p-put on and e-everything thing."

Cody gripped the guy's bony arm and was going to lead him down to the bungalow when he heard Chandler call his name.

"Go," Martin said, his eyes on the kid.

"I'm not leaving J.J."

"I can take care of it. Go talk to your brother."

"You watch him," he said to Martin, handing the kid off. "Get her back inside now. I'll be right down."

Cody jogged over to Chandler. "How's the groom?"

"Better than you, apparently," Chandler replied, thrusting several rolled sheets of paper toward him. "What's with the guns, and where are they taking J.J.?"

Cody's heart stopped as he turned in time to see the taillights of the van blink red before peeling out toward the highway.

Chapter Eighteen

"I need a car!" Cody yelled before kicking the four slashed tires of the Hummer in turn. "A bike! Hell, a skateboard!"

"Calm down," Chandler warned, holding up the keys to his SUV. "I'm parked on the other side of the Inn."

As he ran through the snow, Cody called Seth and gave a description of the van. With Chandler at the wheel once they reached the car, he was able to call his office to start a full-scale search.

"There's an extra coat in the back."

Cody blinked at his brother as if he'd spoken in fluent Farsi. "What?"

"A coat," Chandler prodded. "It's like ten degrees."

Cody hadn't felt the cold. He only felt fear.

WILLY SERVED his purpose and was dropped from the moving van as soon as he'd bound J.J. with rope and given over her gun to Martin.

Martin proceeded to drive another few miles, then pulled off the highway and parked the van in the center of a massive junkyard. "Sorry about this, Barnes." He shoved J.J. off the seat onto the floorboard, then got out and slammed the door.

This was definitely not good. She lay on her side, already feeling the cold starting to affect her, listening as a car engine started. The sound faded, telling her that Martin had abandoned her.

But that didn't make any sense. "Why leave me here?" she wondered aloud. "Why let Willy go? Why no Visnopovs?"

Focus, Barnes. Step one was definitely to hoist herself off the floor. She got a brush burn on her chin from using it to leverage herself by digging it into the upholstery. It took some doing, but she finally managed to wiggle back up onto the seat.

Looking out the front window, she realized that the white van would be hard—if not impossible—to spot from the air. Piles of junk metal, tattered remnants of furniture, and wrecked and twisted cars probably reached two stories high. And they were blanketed with snow, which meant she'd be little more than a dot of white in a sea of white. And she didn't dare risk stumbling out into the snow with her hands tied. Too cold. And cold killed just as effectively as an angry Visnopov.

"The Lord helps those who help themselves," she muttered as she began to kick the plastic console separating the two front seats. On the third kick, the plastic splintered. On the fifth kick, a piece suitable to use as a blade splintered off, flying past her.

J.J. wiggled around, feeling along the crevice between the bench seat and the sliding door. Something sharp pricked her finger. Feeling the outline, she realized it was one of those pointy things used to sink nails.

"An awl," she announced, as if it were a *Jeopardy!* question instead of a momentary way to keep her mind from thinking about her dilemma.

The awl was great if she needed to stab something, but that wasn't the task at hand. She tucked it into the back pocket of her jeans, and kept feeling around the tight crack between the seat and the door. After a few more seconds, she found the makeshift blade. The good news was, all the activity made her perspire. The bad news was, the sun was starting to set. She knew that when the sun dropped, so did the temperature. Quickly.

She set to work sawing through the nylon rope binding her hands. Her steady progress had a calming effect, until she heard the snow crunching under the weight of an approaching car.

The car stopped behind the van. She heard one door open, then a second. *Damn.* At least two. She worked faster at cutting the ropes, as she heard footfalls crunch through the frozen top layer of snow. In the rearview mirror, she monitored their approach. Two men. Dark overcoats. Fully automatic weapons. *Double damn.*

"Nothing so far." Seth's voice crackled over Chandler's speaker phone. Cody cursed and smashed the roll of papers that Chandler had given him against the dashboard. The reverse directory pages provided by Stephenson didn't seem so important anymore.

"I've got choppers up now," Seth said. "Don't worry, Cody, we'll find her."

Alive?

"He couldn't have gotten far," Chandler reasoned just before slamming on the brakes.

Bracing himself as the car fishtailed, Cody spied the form in the center of the road and felt his stomach clench.

"Stop the car. Stop the car!" Before his brother brought the vehicle to a full stop he jumped from the car and ran back, gun trained on the still form.

"Get up."

The only response was a groan.

Cody nudged Willy with his foot. "Get up *now.*"

The young man rolled over. His clothing was shredded, revealing a pretty bad case of road burn on one whole side of his body. He shivered and winced, but managed to open one eye.

"I need a doctor," he croaked.

"Tell me where she is or you'll need a mortician."

"Cody?" Chandler made his name sound like a caution. "He's hurt."

"He's gonna be hurt a lot worse if he doesn't tell me where she is."

"Don't…know," he grunted.

Cody pressed the toe of his boot against the guy's ribs and applied just a bit of pressure.

"Ow! Okay! Okay!"

"Ease off, Cody," Chandler warned, this time more forcefully.

"Yeah, ease off, Cody," the injured guy repeated, his voice stronger now.

"Wrong thing to say," Chandler said pleasantly before giving the guy a swift kick to the stomach.

The guy let out a girlish squeal of pain, then said, "She gave me a hundred bucks to drive the van to the Inn and do whatever the other guy told me to do."

"Names, Willy. I need names," Cody insisted as the rhythmic chop of helicopter blades cut through the evening air. "Now."

"I don't know!" Willy insisted. "The lady that came to the shop seemed...confused."

"Confused?"

"Yep. She had an earpiece in her ear. You know, the kind that connects to a phone? I could hear the guy on the other end. It was either a really bad connection or he had an accent."

"Russian?" Cody's throat clogged with anxiety.

"Maybe. Thick sounding. Not anything I've heard around here."

"Tell me *exactly* what she wanted you to do." Cody knelt to hear the guy over the noise from the hovering chopper.

"It wasn't her. It was him, I think. She seemed really nervous and kept turning back to look around the parking lot."

"Can you describe her?"

"Short brown hair, brown eyes. One arm in a sling."

Lara. Dammit! He'd let her walk out the door. Cody lifted the guy by what was left of his shirt collar. "Tell me everything. Every detail."

"She said he needed a van. Then I hear the Russian guy yelling through the earpiece and she corrects herself. Says it has to be a *white* van." Willy paused to hold his rib cage and cough. "That's when I noticed the guy in the gray van pull up. It made the lady very nervous. Especially when he didn't get out of the van. Just parked at the end of the lot. I figured the Russian guy who was calling the shots was probably in the van and I'm wondering to myself, 'why doesn't he just come in and do the deal?' but he doesn't. He just corrected the lady a few times."

"Like how?"

"Well, the color thing. That was one. Where I was supposed to park at the Inn. She said in the front at first, then I hear him ranting and she changes it to the service road. That was two. She said I should 'put' the tall blonde in the van, then changed it to 'shove.'" Willy's scraped and bloody forehead wrinkled. "Oh, yeah, and she covered the mouthpiece when she told me what to say if I got asked questions before we got the woman in the van."

"What?"

"She lowered her voice and told me to make sure I told you it was a woman who hired me. Then she signed the rental agreement and told me to leave right away."

"Where's the van now?"

"I swear I don't know!" Willy cried, then stiffened as if expecting to be hit.

His fear wasn't completely without merit. The only thing that stopped Cody from pounding the little twerp was time. He wouldn't waste the time. He had to find J.J. before...*no! Don't even think it.* "Where's the rental agreement now?" Cody demanded.

"The original is at the shop. I stuck her copy in the glove compartment of the van."

He turned, but his brother was already dialing. "Get someone to Hank's Truck Rental," Chandler yelled, one finger stuck in his ear as he listened. "Okay, I'll tell him."

He saw Chandler blanch. "What?" Cody asked, his body rigid as dread leeched into every cell.

"They found a body."

"Whose?"

"Steven...Stevens..."

"Stephenson?" Cody asked.

Chandler nodded.

"He is—was—J.J.'s shadow. Where's the body?"

"About three miles from the truck rental place. What do you want to do?"

Cody didn't hesitate. "Find J.J."

Chandler's phone rang and he handed it to Cody. Seth was on the other end. "I've got a guy at the rental place. You should get up here now."

"I know about Stephenson."

"Forget that," Seth insisted. "I'll meet you there in ten minutes."

They were, Cody decided, ten of the longest minutes of his life. It was dark and well below zero by the time Chandler pulled into the group of cars converged on the small combination convenience store, service station, car wash and truck rental establishment.

He found Seth inside, giving instructions to the deputy guarding the elderly couple, seated and handcuffed.

"Willy's grandparents, who own the rental place," Seth explained. "They claim they don't know a thing about the kidnapping. Claim Willy wouldn't do anything like that. And all his juvenile arrests were mistakes. Oh—" Seth's expression conveyed marginally controlled anger "—they won't let us see the rental records without a warrant."

Cody didn't have the time or the inclination to deal gently with loving grandparents in denial. Making his way over to them, he simply told them that Willy had been dumped on the highway by one of the kidnappers and was injured.

"How badly?" the grandmother asked.

Cody flipped out his badge. "I'm a U.S. marshal, ma'am. The witness I was protecting was kidnapped and is about to be murdered."

"Willy wouldn't kill anyone."

"Shut up, Trudy. We won't say nothing until we get a lawyer."

Cody wanted to punch the guy in his protruding beer belly. "Fine. We wait for an attorney. My witness is killed. The actual killers get away. Willy takes the fall alone."

His method worked. Trudy wasn't as stupid as her husband. She quickly directed them to a key in her purse that opened the drawer beneath the cash register.

Finding the rental agreement was easy. Recognizing Lara's handwriting was sad but expected. "So why did she fill this out under her own name?" he asked. "Real name. Real address. Real driver's license number and—"

Cody reread the driver's license number.

"Nine digits?" Seth asked, peering over Cody's shoulder. "What state has a nine-digit license number?"

"Three-zero-five." Cody read the first numbers aloud, allowing a flicker of hope to seep into his thoughts. "It's a phone number."

Cody grabbed the ancient, black plastic rotary phone off the counter and impatiently dialed the number. A woman answered on the first ring. "Who is this?"

"Carol Selznick."

"Lara's mother? Sister? What?"

"Are you Cody Landry?" she asked, surprising him.

"Yes."

"Lara said if you called, I was supposed to tell you the truth." There was a slight pause, then she said, "I'm her wife."

It took Cody a second to wrap his brain around that one. *CLS. Carol and Lara Selznick.* Not "Cabin at Lucky Seven" as he and J.J. had guessed.

"Okay. But that doesn't—"

"Is Lara all right?"

"I don't know," he admitted truthfully. "We've got a bit of a situation here, Miss…Mrs.…*Carol.*"

"I figured as much." There was anxiety and fear in the woman's soft voice. "You are looking for her, aren't you?"

"What did Lara want you to tell me?" Cody asked.

"Someone was blackmailing her."

"I assumed as much, so that's not overly helpful, Carol."

He heard choked sobs on the other end. "It wasn't money," Carol continued, whimpering occasionally. "He made her do things. Things she knew were wrong, but she didn't want to risk my being outed. I'm a teacher, Deputy Landry. In a very conservative private school here in Miami. I'm being considered for tenure and someday, I'd like to be headmistress. If anyone finds out, I'll lose my job. I'm good at it and I—"

"Carol!" he cut in, "was there anything else?"

"Yes. Two things. First, she told me that after this week, Martin and his wife can have a baby."

Cody finally had a inkling of why Martin was involved.

"Lara told me a few months back that Martin's wife needed some sort of special procedure to be able to get pregnant. It's so specialized, their insurance won't cover it." Carol continued between sniffles, "Um, second, and I'm quoting, 'the job is junk.'"

"Excuse me?"

"The job is junk. I know. Weird, because she never says 'junk' and she never complains about the job. But the guy blackmailing her—maybe Martin, I don't know—had tapes of some earlier phone conversations. I figured this was some kind of code she was using when she called today that you'd understand and whoever was tapping our phone wouldn't. Does it help? Will it help you find Lara?"

"I hope so," Cody muttered, his mind running possibilities as he placed the receiver on the cradle. Looking to Chandler and Seth, he asked, "Junk. Mean anything to you?"

"There's a junkyard on Highway 3 west of town."

"How far from the Inn?"

"We passed it on our way here," Seth said. "Three, maybe three and a half miles. Why?"

"I remember the place. I think that's where J.J. might be."

"I'll get the choppers up," Seth said, grabbing the microphone on his shoulder and barking a quick succession of orders.

"I'll drive," Cody announced, snatching the keys from Chandler. "You stay here. You're getting married tomorrow and I—"

"Will be there. Don't be stupid and sentimental, Cody. I'm coming, so get a move on." Chandler dialed his cell phone as they ran to the car.

Cody listened as his brother called for reinforcements. Between Seth's helicopters and deputies and every available Landry brother, they should be able to find J.J.

He only prayed it would be in time.

ONLY A FEW HOURS had passed but J.J. had about another quarter inch of rope to cut through when the door to the van opened. She didn't recognize the men, but she knew them all the same. It was the hats. The Visnopovs loved ushankas. The large fur hats with the long ear flaps were perfect for the harsh Russian climate. And a pretty good idea in Montana, too. She was too scared to be cold.

"Hi, fellas," she greeted, scooting back so that as a last resort, she could at least kick one of them before they shot her. She kept cutting at her bonds, hoping to buy time. "Can I interest you in some scrap metal?"

"Funny girl, this one," the taller of the men said. He smiled, revealing two gaps where teeth should have been.

The smaller one answered in Russian. Doing the translation in her head, she realized it wasn't an answer. Short Russian wanted to know if he needed to lay a tarp in the trunk of the car, or if they just planned on leaving her in the van after they were finished.

Tall Russian said she'd be left with the other one. *What other one?*

Didn't matter. Her hands were free and timing was crucial. J.J. grasped the awl, took a deep breath and let adrenaline take over.

In one action, she kicked Tall Russian in the chin, then leaned forward and stabbed Short Russian in the neck with the awl. Utilizing the momentum of her attack, she pushed through them as their automatic weapons spit wildly into the air.

J.J. bolted around a pile of scrap. She heard cursing, screaming and then the pings of bullets ricocheting off the metal all around her. She crouched down, feeling her way under a rusted car.

There was just enough room for her to half crawl, half crouch beneath a tower of trashed cars and other debris in a seemingly endless tunnel of twisted metal and car carcasses. As she crawled deeper, she felt the jagged edges of something scrape her thigh. Her sweater bunched up, putting her flesh in direct contact with the rough, frozen ground. Bone-deep cold and pain made her shudder. J.J. grit her teeth and forged on. She didn't have her gun, but she picked up a two-by-four piece of metal to use as a crude weapon.

The debris surrounding her got more and more dense, making the makeshift burrow more and more difficult to navigate. But she didn't dare stop moving. She could hear the Russians as they searched for her. Heart pounding, she shifted sideways to squeeze between two rusted truckbeds.

A flash of movement on the other side of the scrap metal made her stop on a dime and hold her breath. One of the Russians was close enough to touch. He stopped, just feet away, his back to her, and looked around. If he turned his head two more inches to the left, they'd be eye to eye.

Then she heard the hum of helicopter blades. Bright, white shafts of light illuminated in the snow and metal.

Rat-tat-tat. Ping-ping-ping. Russians versus helicopter sharpshooter.

She covered her head with her arms as snow and rust rained down on her. As soon as there was a break, she pushed forward.

Emerging cautiously, she kept her back to a sheet of corrugated metal and let her gaze move slowly from left to right. No signs of either man. She pushed away the foot or so of snow blocking her exit, then pulled herself free of the tunnel. She was about to stand when she felt a hand close around her ankle.

He yanked hard. Hard enough that her only choices were to fall to the ground or have her shin snapped like a twig. She must have let out a yelp, something. Because she suddenly heard Cody's voice echoing around her.

She kicked at the death grip around her ankle, half-expecting the Russian to shoot her at any second. Twisting, bucking, trying anything to keep her attacker off balance, J.J. screamed for Cody as she rolled onto her back and looked at the shadowy figure holding her.

The Russian was grunting and cursing, but nothing seemed to lessen his grasp.

Cody skidded around the corner. "J.J.!" he called, slipping as he lost traction in his rush to cover the ten yards or so to where she lay prone in the snow.

"Gun!" she called back.

The beam from the helicopter that had been following him, spotted J.J., allowing him to see that someone had her ankle in one hand. Through the tangled web of metal, he saw the outline of a semiautomatic snaking through in order for her captor to get off a clean shot. At that range, there was no way she'd survive it.

"J.J.!" he yelled, getting her attention for the split second it took to toss her his gun.

It took five rounds before the fingers clutching her ankle released.

She was breathing so heavily that she almost couldn't speak when Cody fell to her side and gathered her against him. Closing her eyes briefly, she nuzzled close to him, drinking in the comfort of his smell and relishing the safety of being in his arms.

Then she heard it. A brief creaking sound above them. Reacting to the sight of the Short Russian, his face and neck drenched with his own blood, poised and ready to fire from his high perch, she shoved Cody out of the way and took aim.

The snow exploded around them as bullets slammed into the ground. It was quick. Then it was over. She had only one thought. Cody!

He lay on his back, eyes closed, lips tight, cheeks hollow. Scrambling to her knees, J.J. began frantically checking him for wounds. She couldn't find any.

"Talk to me," she pleaded, practically shaking him. "Cody, where does it hurt?"

One eye struggled to open as he pointed to his chest. "Here."

Oh, Lord. He could barely talk. She ripped off the top

two buttons of his coat, searching with hands and eyes for blood, a bullet hole, an entry point, but still couldn't find the wound.

"I'm going to have to roll you over." She started to slip her hands beneath him when she saw the flicker of a smile at the edge of his lips. "You're faking?" she accused.

"No, my chest does hurt. You knocked the wind out of me when you flipped me."

"Baby."

"And—" he paused to brush her lips with a kiss "—it hurts because you won't admit that you love me."

She thought about it. Really, really thought about it. Nope. Not yet. "Grow from the pain," she told him, kissing him quickly when she heard the thunder of people running in their direction.

She frowned. "Did you call in the National Guard or something?"

He pointed toward the approaching group. "I don't need the Guard. I have Landrys."

"How nice for you."

His expression stilled. "I *have* them, but I *want* you. I love you, J.J."

She pressed her lips to his forehead and said, "I know."

Epilogue

"Nice service," J.J. said when Cody was finally released by the photographer and able to join her near the fireplace.

"Nice dress," he practically purred against her ear.

"You bought it," she said, quelling the urge to twirl around to show off the perfect way it fit. "I thought it was the least I could do."

"What have you been up to all day?" he asked. "I kept calling your room leaving voice mails."

"I was getting to know Cade's wife, Barbara."

"Lovely woman. In advertising, right?"

J.J. slipped her hand around his waist as she took a flute of champagne from a passing waiter. She drank it a little too quickly.

"I believe you're supposed to sip that," Cody teased, the firelight reflecting in his dark eyes.

"Well, I've had a rough twenty-four hours."

He gave her a gentle squeeze. "It's over."

"Not completely," she told him. "The bureau can't find anything to link Visnopov directly to the two guys from the junkyard. With both of them dead, there's no one to flip."

"No, I guess not," Cody agreed. "CSIs found Lara's body at the junkyard. Preliminary ballistics indicate she was killed by the Russians. So was your field agent, Stephenson."

She lifted her palm to his cheek. "I'm sorry, Cody, I know you didn't want to believe your team was involved. Any word on Martin?"

He rubbed her back as he gazed into the fire. "I got the call a little while before the wedding. They found him at the airport in Helena. He wrote a note before he killed himself."

Hearing his sharp intake of breath made her heart hurt.

"It doesn't help your case much," he said, almost apologetically. "Martin only owned up to taking cash from the mob—no names—for his wife's fertility treatment. And he did his best to clear Lara's name. Laid out how he used her. Had her rig the snowmobile. Rent the truck. I guess when Martin told Lara about his baby troubles, she confided her sexual orientation. When the mob approached Martin, he used it to coerce her into helping him."

"I'm sorry."

"Not your fault. No one's fault but Martin's. I just wish he would have given you something that would have helped your case against the Visnopovs."

They stood together quietly for several minutes, listening to the harpist. She could tell the music relaxed Cody, but it had the opposite effect on her.

She grabbed another flute of champagne and again, she gulped, rather than sipped.

Cody arched one brow questioningly. "Problem?"

She nodded. "I wasn't really going to do this here."

"Do what."

Setting the glass on the mantle, she took Cody by the hand and led him into a semiprivate alcove near the back of the room. "I've got something important to tell you."

Finally, he thought.

"I'm leaving the bureau."

"What?"

"I was always prepared for the dangers associated with my job. I wasn't ready for my job becoming the danger," she said. "My superiors were completely comfortable getting me killed to make the case. That's a little more than I'm willing to do. I'll testify once the grand jury convenes, but after that…"

"So, do you have any ideas?"

She nodded. "That's why I spoke to Barbara today."

"You're going from the FBI to advertising?" He'd either had too much to drink or not enough. Bottom line, she was making no sense.

"No. I just wanted the name of a printer who could work something up spur of the moment."

"So…you're going into printing?"

"No." She reached into the small clutch dangling from her incredibly sexy wrist and pulled out a single business card. "I was thinking of this."

He took the card and read it. "Landry Investigations and Security Consultants." Slowly he lifted his eyes and met hers. "Who is the Landry on this card?"

"You, of course," she told him, her expression solemn as she slipped her arms around his neck. "It would mean leaving the Marshal Service."

"Why would I want to do that?"

"To be near your family, for one thing."

"That's a plus." He stepped into her, feeling the outline of her body through the thin, clingy fabric of the dress. They fit perfectly. "Why else?"

"You're great with security issues. You're well connected and you can get things done."

"True." He kissed her neck and enjoyed the little catch in her breath. "So why investigations *and* security? My forte is really security."

"Then you'd need someone like…maybe…a former FBI agent to handle those matters."

"Know anyone in Montana that fits the bill?"

"Me. I could be persuaded to work for you."

"Not interested." He smiled against her throat when he felt her stiffen in his arms.

"But I thought…you said…you claimed…"

Cupping her face in his hands, he looked directly into her eyes and said, "Not *for* me, J.J., *with* me. And only if you'll marry me."

She smiled. "That was going to be my line. That's why I kept seeking fortitude in the champagne."

"I don't think it will work, J.J.," he told her, his expression somber.

"Why?"

"Because you haven't told me that you love me."

"I love you."

"And because you haven't told me that you'll marry me."

"I will."

He kissed her for a long, long time. Leaving her

breathless. Wanting nothing more than to skip the meal and go up to her room.

"Oh, another thing…" J.J. opened her small clutch and handed him a folded piece of paper.

He gave her a puzzled look as he opened it. Turned it over. "There's nothing on it but a date."

"It's symbolic."

His lips quirked. "OK. I'll bite. Symbolic of what?"

"A doctor's note. Since Dr. Landry wanted to make sure we…refrained until the date circled. Then we're free to—"

He wrapped his arms around her and pressed a kiss to her smiling mouth before saying, "Should we talk about kids?"

"We'll have some."

"You don't hold back, do you, J.J.?"

"I do," she insisted, pretending to get huffy. "I held back the fact that we have our first client."

"Who?"

"I don't want to tell you yet. Do you love me?"

"Yes. And I want to be told. Now."

"Are you going to be all demanding and macho on me?" she asked. "Because we both know I'm capable of dropping you like a bad habit."

"J.J., I love you. I want to marry you. I want to build a life with you here. I want to have children with you. I want to grow old with you. There, see? Everything right out on the table. Your turn. Who's the client?"

"You."

"Me?"

"Consider it my engagement present, Cody." She held his gaze. "I asked Stephenson to do a little digging for me. Thanks to him, I might have a lead on your parents."

* * * * *

Don't miss Shane's story when
THE LAST LANDRY hits shelves
March 2006 from Harlequin Intrigue.

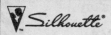

INTRIGUE

Don't miss this first title in Lori L. Harris's
exciting new Harlequin Intrigue series—

THE BLADE BROTHERS
OF COUGAR COUNTY

TARGETED

(Harlequin Intrigue #901)

BY LORI L. HARRIS

On sale February 2006

Alec Blade and Katie Carroll think they can start
fresh in Cougar County. Each hopes to bury the
unresolved events of their violent pasts. But they
soon learn just how mistaken they are when a
faceless menace reappears in their lives. Suddenly
it isn't a matter of outrunning the past. Now they
have to survive long enough to have a future.

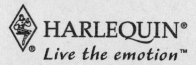

HARLEQUIN®
Live the emotion™